Double Cross Dead

A 1920s historical mystery

A Dora and Rex Mystery
Book 4

Lynn Morrison

Marketing Chair Press

Cover design by DLR Cover Designs

Published by

The Marketing Chair Press, Oxford, England

LynnMorrisonWriter.com

Print ISBN: 978-1-7392632-4-9

Contents

To my parents, Ken and Joyce - thanks for always being ready to lend a hand.

Chapter 1
The Secret Meeting

Lord Reginald Bankes-Fernsby discarded his empty champagne glass onto the tray of a passing footman. He stood on the edge of a cluster of men his age, only half-listening to the discussion. Truth be told, it hardly mattered what any of his peers said. There was only one person worth paying attention to in the crowded ballroom, and she was currently spinning around on the dance floor.

Rex noted the other men who, like himself, couldn't take their eyes off Theodora Laurent. Despite the staid colour of her gown, Dora stood out. With her red-gold hair, she shone like a brightly coloured peacock amongst the pale grey doves of London's upper class set. Rex had heard more than one overbearing mother warn their marriage-hunting daughters to steer clear of the notorious femme fatale.

The only problem with that advice was that the men, single or otherwise, followed at her heels. They fell in line like dogs obeying their master, clinging desperately to the hope that she might grace them with her favour.

In fact, Rex was likely the only red-blooded, single man

there who hadn't begged her for a space on her dance card. That wasn't because of any lack of affection on his part.

Quite the opposite.

No matter which man held her in his arms, Dora's eyes had a habit of seeking Rex. Just now, she'd glanced his way when she twirled past, raising her eyebrows in a silent request for help. He didn't need to be a mind-reader to recognise his cue to step in.

He didn't bother to wait for the tune to end. Instead, without a word of by your leave, he crossed the floor and tapped Dora's partner on his shoulder. "Pardon my tardiness, but I believe this dance is mine."

The distinguished gentleman, a titled lord who owned half the land in Wiltshire, opened his mouth to argue, but stopped short when he saw whom he faced. Although there were no marriage bonds tying Dora and Rex together, their frequent appearances in the gossip rags made it clear their lives were intertwined.

Dora took advantage of the man's discomfort, to slip free of his loose hold. She turned to Rex, stepping into his embrace, and trailed a finger along the length of starched white fabric beneath his bowtie. "And here I thought you'd forgotten about me."

Rex tossed back his head and laughed at her ridiculous statement before launching into the measured steps of the waltz. "Something tells me that even if I lost my memory entirely, the vision of you would remain."

Dora gave him a warm smile, letting him know how much he'd pleased her. It wasn't until the previous dance partner left the floor that Dora's smile slipped from her face. As they moved in time to the strains of the violins, Dora pinched his arm.

"What was that for?" Rex grunted, his arm smarting.

"I expected you sooner. My toes will be bruised for the next week. And don't get me started on his halitosis. Does the man dine exclusively on garlic and anchovies?"

2

Rex barely held on to his self-restraint. "You taught me to exploit every opportunity to weaken my foe. How am I ever meant to get one-up on you if I let occasions like this one pass me by?"

"Promises, promises, darling." She punctuated her bold statement with a wink.

Unfortunately, standing in the middle of the Grand Reception room in Windsor Castle, Rex was unable to do more than let his imagination run wild. He held Dora close, or as near as he dared, given his grandmother's watchful gaze. Although she approved of their burgeoning relationship, even she drew the line at flaunting it in front of the king and queen.

Tonight, the highest echelons of Britain's upper class had gathered to celebrate a milestone in the lives of the royal family. From the heir to the throne down to the knights and earls, no one got through the castle gates without a title to their name or a lifelong friendship with the reigning monarchs.

No one, that is, except Theodora Laurent.

Rex had caught more than one sneer aimed in his partner's direction. The same society mavens who balked at her presence would welcome her with open arms if they knew who she really was. However, Dora's cover was fully in place. With her light French accent and daring Parisian gown, she was a far cry from the young Lady Dorothy Cavendish who'd once played in the castle grounds.

Rex chanced a glance toward the monarchs seated on velvet-upholstered, gilded thrones at the end of the room. King George V and Queen Mary rarely engaged in more than the perfunctory opening dance at events such as these. The king's reputation for strictness was well known. Even now, the king glowered at the swirling skirts spinning past. His drooping salt and pepper moustache emphasised his frown. Queen Mary did her best to remain more upbeat, conveying a smile more appropriate to the celebratory occasion.

After all, it wasn't often that one's son got engaged.

They'd likely have preferred that their older son be the one to settle down. However, Edward, Prince of Wales and heir to the throne, showcased a nimbleness both on and off the dance floor. His primary passions were racing, dancing, and gambling. It was no wonder Rex's friend Lord Clark counted him as a close acquaintance. The two men revelled in their status as proud bachelors.

His younger brother Albert, known to his friends as Bertie, was on the flip-side of the coin. Shy, studious, and devoted to his wife-to-be.

Tonight, several hundred guests gathered at Windsor Castle to raise a toast to the couple. Prince Bertie had finally succeeded in getting Lady Elizabeth Bowes-Lyon to accept his offer of marriage. Although Bertie was the spare, at least he was setting a good example of doing his duty to the family legacy.

Not that Edward paid his brother any attention. The prince was too busy tossing back glasses of champagne to notice.

Rex let his gaze drift around the dance floor until a sharp tug on his sleeve reminded him of the woman in his arms.

"This is the first time a man has dared to daydream while dancing with me," Dora chided, giving him a stern look. "Stop worrying."

"I wasn't worrying," Rex replied. He forced his mouth into a grin and squeezed her hand.

"Were you counting steps? This is exactly why I hate this dance. So many rules, so little freedom to lose yourself in the music. What do you think our monarchs would do if I asked the band to play a foxtrot? At least then I could enjoy sidling closer to your muscular physique."

Rex's heart skipped a beat. He could not say whether that

was out of excitement or fear. Fortunately, their timeline dictated that this would be their last dance. Unlike the dancers around them, Rex and Dora were there on assignment.

Rex focused on keeping his steps in time with the music, while counting down until the end of the tune. When the last notes of the violins hung in the air, he shifted around until he and Dora had an unobstructed view of Prince Bertie.

A middle-aged man, dressed impeccably in black tie and tails, slid into place behind the younger prince. Bertie glanced over his shoulder and froze in place. He might be third in line for the throne, but even Bertie knew to pay attention when Lord Audley, Duke of Montagu, whispered in his ear.

Bertie's brow scrunched. Rex read the word on his lips. "Now?"

Lord Audley nodded. Bertie gave him a bewildered glance, but did as he was told. He had a quiet word with Lady Elizabeth and then excused himself from the room.

Thus far, the plan had proceeded without a hitch.

Lord Audley watched Prince Bertie make his way through the crowd. Only when the prince had left the room did he turn back and give Rex a subtle nod.

That was Rex's cue to move.

"All this movement has caused me to work up a sweat. I don't suppose you'd like to accompany me for a walk outside while I catch a breath of air?"

Dora fanned herself. "I'm up for taking a break, but only if you promise to keep me from catching a chill." She fluttered her lashes.

"Have I ever let you down?" Rex didn't wait for an answer. He wrapped an arm around her slender waist and led her toward the exit to the terrace.

The frosty night air nearly took his breath away. Thankfully, their path took them only a few doors down and back inside again. Rex glimpsed Prince Bertie when he walked past the entrance to their side corridor.

Without a word, Rex and Dora picked up their pace as they hurried along the deep carpet runner. It muffled their steps, allowing them to move at a steady clip. Although they knew exactly where the prince was headed, they needed to time their arrival to less than a moment after his.

The castle corridors were no less glamorous than the myriad of state rooms that stood off of them. Silk wallpaper embossed with classic patterns covered the walls. The artwork included paintings of past monarchs and landscapes of the British realm, reminding visitors of their leaders and wide influence. Dora and Rex passed more than one curio cabinet displaying a fraction of the royals' immense collection of silver, gold, and fine china.

If the pair hadn't grown up in the lap of luxury, they might have slowed to look.

Two masculine voices caught their attention. Rex exchanged a glance with Dora. Was there someone else involved? She shook her head.

Rex stopped short of the turn into the next hallway. He peered around the corner. Further along, as expected, walked Prince Bertie. He wasn't alone. An ebony-haired gentleman in evening attire matched the prince's sedate pace.

The two men, both narrow of frame and of similar heights, had their heads close together. It took Rex a moment to determine the identity of the other man. It was Thomas Liddell, one of Bertie's closest friends.

And, possibly, the source of malicious threats against the crown.

He tamped down his impulse to call out the man's name. The men were deep in conversation, so engrossed they paid no mind to anyone following behind. Bertie was still moving in the right direction.

Rex had to trust that Bertie would find a way to disentangle himself before he arrived at his destination. He offered Dora his hand and took comfort as her fingers slid between his. Despite them both wearing gloves, intertwining their fingers felt oddly sensual. Rex focused on the conversation ahead to keep his mind from wandering off.

"... Worried about Tabitha," Liddell said.

"Hugh wouldn't..." Bertie replied.

"Then what would it hurt to ask..." Liddell countered.

Try as he might, Rex couldn't hear more than a scrap here and there. What floated his way did little to explain why Thomas Liddell sought urgent council from his friend. It was the night of the man's engagement. Surely there was a better time and place for discussing personal problems?

Bertie must have agreed. He held up a hand to stop Liddell's pleading. "... Talk about this later?"

Thomas Liddell wasn't taking no for an answer.

Rex ran through the mental calculations. Prince Bertie had to arrive in the Semi-State room within the next few minutes. Rex or Dora could call out Thomas's name and hope he alone stopped.

But what if Prince Bertie lingered behind?

Either way, there was still the issue of keeping close to the prince himself. How would Dora or Rex explain why they needed to follow Prince Bertie to a private meeting? Or anywhere, for that matter. They barely knew the man.

Everything rested on getting their timing exactly right. Planning a secret rendezvous in one of the most heavily guarded properties in England wasn't exactly easy. Add in several hundred of the royals' closest acquaintances, time-sensitive messages, and yards of corridors... Was it any wonder they'd encountered a wrinkle?

There was nothing for it. Still, Rex looked Dora's way to see if she had any bright ideas. Her firm expression and pure focus on the backs of the two men suggested she did not.

Prince Bertie and Thomas Liddell followed the corridor around another turn. Rex and Dora slowed their pace even further.

The meeting point was just around the corner. The couple stood perfectly still and pretended to stare up at a painting on the wall. In reality, they hardly dared to breathe as they listened for the scrape of the door.

"Thomas, I'm afraid I must ask you to wait out here," Bertie said to his friend.

"Why?"

"Do you require an explanation?" Bertie asked, his voice rising. "I've promised to do as you asked, but at the moment, I have a more urgent issue on my plate. You can wait over there, if you'd like. Or go back to the ballroom. I'll find you later."

Rex wished he could see Thomas's face, but he didn't dare edge closer. He squeezed Dora's hand.

"You're acting strange. I'll sit until you're done."

The tightness in Rex's chest eased a notch.

The doorknob gave a faint rattle when Bertie turned it. The sound paled compared to the harsh gasp and cry that followed.

Dora launched around the corner, dragging Rex by his hand. There was no sign of the prince. Thomas stood in the hallway with his mouth hanging open.

Rex sped around Dora and nudged Thomas aside. He wanted a clear view of the scene.

A red Aubusson rug covered the stone floor. Velvet curtains in a matching shade covered the floor to ceiling windows lining the far wall.

The deep crimson blood staining the dead man's chest almost appeared to be part of the design.

Rex, Dora, and Thomas rushed into the room. Prince Bertie had his hands up as he pleaded with the killer.

"Put the knife down, man. There's no reason to hurt anyone else."

Lord Clark Kenworthy, Rex's best friend, was as pale as the white Leavers lace throw draped across the back of the deep rose sofa. He glanced down at his hand and swayed when he caught sight of the dagger clutched in his own fist.

"I didn't! It wasn't me!"

Despite his desperate entreaties, the bloodstained dagger in his glove-covered right hand told a very different story.

Chapter 2
The Assignment

T WO DAYS EARLIER
Dora shimmied up the trunk of the oak tree, testing the strength of the branches on her way. The lowest ones proved to be too weak to support her weight, but the higher ones would do.

"Come on," she urged her partner-in-crime in a hoarse whisper.

Rex stood at the base of the tree and stared up incredulously. "Why are we scaling a tree when Lord Audley gave us the key to the gate?"

"Because next time we might not be so lucky. What's the problem, Rexy darling? Worried about getting a few leaves on your hair?"

Rex was probably worrying about what his valet Brantley would say if Rex ripped his trousers. That argument, however, wasn't going to sway Dora. She smiled in satisfaction when he tugged his gloves firmly into place and raised his arms.

In silence, hiding in the treetop, they surveyed the narrow garden behind the London townhouse. Other than an iron table and four chairs, it was devoid of furniture. This wasn't the home of someone who enjoyed the outdoors. Perhaps that was being unfair. Given it was the depths of winter, a narrow patch of garden held little appeal on the best of days.

"Good thing we aren't sneaking in. Other than the spot of shadow below us, the rest of the garden is well lit."

"We'll stick to the edges, where the light is weak," Dora said. "Audley expects us to use the gate over there. We still have a chance of catching him off guard."

She crawled along the sturdiest branch and then swung down to land on her feet. They kept low to the ground until they reached the back of the house. Audley sat in a chair near the fire, smoking a cigar. Dora rapped on the window and chuckled when he startled at the noise. Satisfied she'd once again proved her skills, she led Rex to the door and went inside.

"Must you always be so mischievous?" Audley asked. "I keep expecting you to outgrow your devilish antics."

"Mind your tongue!" Dora countered. "The day I behave will be the day they lower my body into the ground."

"Which is hopefully many, many years away," Rex added, smoothing the waters.

Mollified, Dora claimed the small sofa and patted the seat next to her. After Rex sat, she turned to Lord Audley. "Your mistress's abode is not our normal meeting point. Things must be getting desperate if we need this level of secrecy."

"Indeed." Audley leaned over and picked up a white envelope. He handed it to Dora and Rex.

Dora caught her breath when she spied his name and address typed on the front. She didn't need to open the envelope to know what was inside.

"Our informant is back again?"

"This time with an ultimatum. Now that they've established their bonafides, they want me to arrange for a private conversation with Prince Bertie," Audley replied. He puffed on his cigar and blew smoke rings in the air. Despite his appearance of nonchalance, Dora wasn't fooled.

"Where?"

"At the prince's engagement party in two nights' time. I'll say no, of course. It's out of the question."

Dora's stomach lurched. While she understood Audley's decision, it didn't sit right. "Give us one more night out with Prince Edward and his crowd. I'm sure the informant must be within his inner circle. It's the only thing that makes sense."

"None of this makes sense, and no amount of time is going to clear it up." Rex took the envelope from Dora's hand and handed it back to their mentor. "What will you do now? Tell Prince Bertie? Tell the king?"

Lord Audley blanched at the latter suggestion. "Certainly not the king. He has no sense of humour. If this is a joke played in poor taste, I don't want some poor sod to end up in the Tower. I'll have to tell Bertie and see what he wants to do. I hate this as much as the two of you, but we have no control over the situation. We have no way of getting a message back to our informant. Despite your best efforts, we still have no clue as to their identity."

Therein lay the crux of their problems. Three weeks earlier, the first anonymous letter arrived in the post. The sender proclaimed that one or more of Prince Bertie's closest friends plotted against him. Lord Audley had disregarded the message as nonsense.

But then, a second one arrived.

The subsequent letter included information on the royal family that only an insider would know. The sender told Lord Audley to put a coded message in the Times classifieds.

He did so. Two more messages were sent to emphasise the gravity of the situation without disclosing any identifiable information.

At that point, Lord Audley had to admit that he was out of his depth. Although he was the country's leading expert on foreign affairs, his remit did not include matters closer to home. He needed help, and there was only one man capable of offering it.

Lord Cavendish, the Duke of Dorset. Dora's father.

Thus, Lord Cavendish became a begrudging accomplice in the search for the identity of the anonymous informant. It was a delicate task requiring an expert spy... Or two, in this case.

He agreed to let Dora and Rex spy upon their fellow Englishmen. Their goal was twofold — out the informant and discover who was plotting against Prince Bertie.

Dora and Rex readily volunteered to undertake the mission. Given Prince Bertie's introverted nature, they began with his brother. Prince Edward was more than happy to have the famous Theodora Laurent and her beau Lord Rex join his entourage of pleasure seekers. Perhaps with more time, their plan of slowly working their way into Bertie's confidence via his brother would have worked.

However, the informant wasn't willing to wait.

Dora had some questions. "Did the letter ask you to arrange an invitation to the event?"

Lord Audley cocked his head to the side. "No. I hadn't thought about it, but it proves the individual is high-placed."

Dora had been so focused on uncovering the name of the informant that she'd overlooked something. If their informant had enough clout to get inside the castle during a high-profile event, why couldn't they approach the prince on their own?

Dora turned to the men. "Why is the informant going to all this trouble?"

"You think I haven't asked myself the same question?" asked Lord Audley. "That's all I've done since the second letter arrived and I realised this person was serious. If there is a reasonable answer, it eludes me."

Dora settled against the back of the sofa and crossed her arms. She drummed her fingers and let her mind wander. In times such as these, she usually relied upon the stores of knowledge she'd gained from reading books over the years. However, nothing in her normal repertoire seemed relevant. Machiavelli would no doubt declare this informant a threat to the prince's safety. Socrates would take her question, turn it around, and serve it right back to her. If she thought hard enough, she'd arrive at the answer on her own.

Unfortunately, the Socratic method wasn't drawing out any solutions.

If books were of no help, then she'd have to rely upon her second-best source of information — people.

She glanced at the two men in the room. Someone brave and outgoing like them wouldn't bother sending notes to a third party. If Dora had a message to convey, she'd do it herself.

Equally, she excluded all the timid people she'd met in her life. To them, even sending an anonymous letter would seem risky.

Therefore, it had to be someone who fell in the middle of the spectrum of personalities.

Someone like her brother Will.

A memory sprang to mind.

It was the summer after her eighth birthday. The family had gone for an extended visit to the seaside with her aunt and uncle. Cousin Bartholomew, deemed an acceptable playmate given their close ages, was a first-rate bully. Dora had been ready to wallop him in the nose as soon as Nanny turned her back, but Will had suggested an alternative.

"You can't hit him because then you'll end up in trouble, Dora!" Will had pointed out in a far too reasonable tone. "If we snitch and that barbarian finds out, things will only get worse."

"What do you suggest we do?"

Will had pulled a scrap of paper and a broken stub of a pencil from his pocket. "We'll leave Nanny a note. Make it look like it is from one of the servants. She can catch him in the act. He'll have no one to blame but himself, and we'll get off scot-free."

Dora hadn't been able to argue with his logic back then. It held up just as well now. She uncrossed her arms and sat up. "I've changed my mind. We need to make sure that meeting happens."

Lord Audley choked, causing smoke to stream from his nostrils. While he regained control, Rex asked Dora to clue them in on how and why she'd arrived at that conclusion.

"Our only reason for saying no is fear for Bertie's safety. But let me ask you this." She turned to face Rex. "If you harboured ill-intentions toward a member of England's ruling family, who is the last person you'd want to find out?"

Rex's eyes shifted from Dora's face to Lord Audley's. Lord Audley's reputation as a powerhouse problem-solver was well known.

"Exactly. Same goes for someone playing a joke. Our Lord Audley is known for many things, but his sense of humour isn't one of them. Therefore, we must assume that this person is deadly serious and not a risk. Can either of you find fault with my logic?"

Neither man raised any concerns.

Lord Audley removed the cigar from his mouth and stubbed it out in a nearby ashtray. "Let's get down to the business of planning."

Dora nudged Rex with her elbow and murmured, "Methinks he's trying to hustle us out the door."

"Well, we are at his mistress's home..."

Lord Audley cleared his throat much louder than strictly required, putting a stop to their chatter. "How familiar are you two with the layout of Windsor Castle?"

"I've committed the floor plan to memory," Dora answered automatically.

"And yet, you haven't seen fit to assign me that homework," Rex pointed out. "I have vague recollections from previous visits, but I'm sure my memories pale in comparison to Dora's. I can study tomorrow."

"I'll do you one better," Audley said, waving off the suggestion. "I'll need to arrange for invitations. You can pop round the morning before the big event to collect them. That will give you an excuse to get past the gate. From there, I'll have a guard show you the parts of the castle that aren't open to the public."

"That leaves me free to shop for a dress..."

Dora barely got the words out before Lord Audley called her to a halt.

"Your shopping trip must wait. I still want you to come up with a plan for protecting the prince."

Dora bit back her retort.

"Even if we don't think our anonymous informant is a threat, there is still the matter of his inner circle. We need to keep an eye on him at all times. Subtlety is key. I can only arrange for so many guards to be onsite during the party, and a few in the ballroom itself."

Dora tapped her chin. "What if we disguise extra guards as servants?"

"I like your way of thinking. I presume you have someone in mind?"

"I do," she answered, ticking the names off her fingers. "Harris has sufficient training in both roles to pull them off convincingly." Her smile widened when Audley gave a nod of approval.

Security settled, she was once again free to focus on finding the perfect dress. It wasn't a matter of style so much as need. For the first time ever, Theodora Laurent was going to fade into the background.

Chapter 3
Scoping Out the Scene

Rex admired the view of Windsor Castle through the front windscreen of his shiny black Rolls-Royce. Despite unseasonably cold temperatures, the sun hung high in the sky, bathing the castle walls with a warm glow.

He followed the road that encircled the hill, keeping a careful eye on the many pedestrians on the crowded pavement near the tourist shops. Windsor was a strange juxtaposition, where everyday life sat on one side of the narrow, winding road and the thick stone castle walls on the other. In medieval times, the townspeople had chosen to build their lives only steps away from the safety of the castle guard. What had once been bakeries and market stalls now played host to storefronts. Instead of food and drink, he spotted postcards, cheap trinkets, and Union flags, all offered for sale to the visiting tourists.

The old cobblestone road hadn't been designed with cars in mind. Rex sounded his horn when a gaggle of schoolgirls strayed into the street. Even going as slowly as he was, it still wasn't safe for them to cross without looking. No one, however, was paying any attention to the cars. Everyone was there for one sight only — that of the castle sitting on the hill.

Built nearly a thousand years earlier, Windsor Castle had begun its life as a defensive fortress. The mott and bailey design went through multiple reconstructions and expansions, eventually becoming a palace fit for the royal family to host state visitors. Since Queen Victoria had opened a small section of the castle to the public, thousands of people had been given the opportunity to see how the royals lived.

Perhaps it was for that reason that the current king and queen typically chose to spend their days at one of their other palaces. Far away from the public eye, the young princes and princesses experienced a somewhat normal childhood. Now, however, those children were well into adulthood. The occasion of a royal engagement party required the family to make use of Windsor's illustrious setting.

The Royal Standard swayed in the breeze at the top of the mast above the castle, indicating that the royals were in residence. A line of visitors queued outside the castle gates, waiting for their turn to visit the public areas of the royal estate. Many turned to watch Rex drive past in his expensive Rolls-Royce Phantom. He squirmed in his seat, unaccustomed to attracting so much attention. Things only got worse when he arrived at the top of the hill and found a delivery lorry blocking the main entrance to the castle car park.

A guard hurried over to Rex's window. After confirming Rex's name was on the guest list, the guard asked him to wait for a moment while the driver finished unloading the delivery. Rex had no choice but to cool his heels inside his car.

Rex lowered his window an inch and took a breath of the fresh air. A flash of light blinded him for a second. It was a tourist, snapping a photo. Rex didn't know whether to frown or to wave. Was this how zoo animals felt?

A high-pitched voice caught Rex's ear. "Mary, look over there. I think that's him."

"Him who?" Another female voice answered. "With a fancy car like that, he's a toff for sure. Do you think he's a friend of the prince?"

"Maybe, but that isn't what I meant. Look here."

Rex shifted his head slowly until he caught a glimpse of the two women in his side mirror. One of them pulled a newspaper from her bag and opened it up. She pointed excitedly at the page.

"I knew it. It has to be him. Lord Rex!"

Rex's cheeks flamed in embarrassment. He turned back to glare at the lorry. The driver was climbing inside, but didn't appear to be in any hurry. Rex felt like a monkey in a cage, but that was hardly a cause of concern for the lorry driver.

The women's voices piped back up.

"He's very handsome, isn't he?"

"Think he'll take me for a spin in that posh car of his if I ask nicely?"

Rex gripped onto the steering wheel and began praying for an escape. It turned out, however, that he wasn't the primary focus of the women's admiration.

"Forget about him, Molly. I'm more interested in meeting the dame on his arm in that photo. Miss Theodora Laurent. No title to her name, but the toffs fawn over her as though she were the queen herself. I'd like to know her secret to capturing the interest of the highest lords in the land."

Molly threw back her head and roared with laughter. "Nancy, you are a hoot. You can find the answer to that question just by looking at her picture."

The lorry driver finally pulled forward, clearing the way for Rex to drive onto the castle grounds. His initial embarrassment had given way to amusement. Although the old saying declared *a picture was worth a thousand words*, when it came to Dora, not even the greatest artist in the world could do justice to her secrets.

He was still chuckling when he walked through the arched opening in the castle walls. He spied a middle-aged woman in a severe black dress and matching dour expression waiting for him beside a door in the Lower Ward. Unlike the ladies outside, this woman was decidedly less impressed by Lord Rex. As the private secretary to the Crown Prince, the second son of an Earl hardly warranted her notice.

He raised a hand and gave a friendly wave. At his acknowledgement, the woman unbent enough to allow a small smile to cross her lips.

"Good afternoon, Lord Reginald. I appreciate you saving me a trip into London."

"It was my pleasure. Getting away from the big smoke, even for a short while, does one good. Besides, I studied over there." Rex pointed in the direction of Eton. "Despite the proximity, I confess I've spent little time at the castle."

"That explains why Lord Audley asked me to arrange for a warden to show you around. Before I take you to him, I don't want to forget to pass this along." The woman handed Rex a cream-coloured envelope.

Rex checked that both his and Dora's names were inscribed across the front. He didn't need to break the royal seal on the back to know what was inside. Lord Audley had indeed come through with a last-minute invitation to the engagement fete. Thus reassured, Rex tucked it into his coat pocket. "The most coveted invitation in the land — I fear I will be in Lord Audley's debt for a long while."

"I have no doubts about that," the Prince's secretary agreed. "But rest assured, you made a wise choice. I wouldn't have gone to the trouble of arranging last-minute invitations for anyone else."

That caught Rex off-guard. "I wasn't aware that Lord Audley and Prince Edward were very close."

If anything, he'd have expected just the opposite. Audley had little patience for the playboy prince.

"They are far from friends, that's for sure. But given the number of times Lord Audley has got Prince Edward out of the scrape, adding a couple of names to the guest list was the least I could do." She flipped over the page on her clipboard, revealing another envelope underneath. "I don't suppose you expect to see Lord Audley today. Before the ball, I mean."

Rex wasn't due to meet with the man, but when he spotted the typed name on the front of the envelope, he rearranged his plans. It was exactly like the anonymous messages Audley had received. He held out his hand. "As a matter of fact, I am going to stop by his home when I get back to London. I have a small gift of thanks to drop off. Shall I tell him this is a message from you or from Prince Edward?"

Rex waited with bated breath for an answer. Was it possible they would learn the identity of their anonymous informant before the night had even begun?

The woman gave a small shake of her head. "Neither. I found the letter sitting on my desk this morning. I had planned to pass it along tonight, but since you're here now, I'll let you do the honours." She handed Rex the envelope, completely unaware of the significance.

Rex tilted the envelope enough to see it was sealed shut. He could hardly open it here, but equally, he didn't dare wait. He needed a moment of privacy.

"Before I take off with the warden, is there a telephone I can use? I promised to phone Theodora as soon as I got inside. She said she wouldn't believe we had an invitation until I had them in my hand."

The woman's face softened for a moment. "You can use the

one in my office. I'll fetch the warden and have him wait outside until you're ready."

Rex could barely contain his excitement while he followed her into the office space. Built into a section of the outer wall, it had likely served as a guards' station in days of yore. Now, the whitewashed walls and electric lights illuminated a line of small offices. The click and clatter of busy typewriters muffled their steps on the stone floor.

No sooner had the door shut behind the secretary than Rex grabbed a letter opener from the top of her desk and slit open the envelope. Inside was a sheet of paper with a single line of text.

Semi-State room. Midnight.

The missing time and location.

This information was invaluable. Rex didn't want to wait until he was back in London to communicate the news. He lifted the handset and asked the operator to connect him to Dora's number. He'd have to be clever in his phrasing, but he trusted Dora would be able to interpret his coded words.

Harris answered the call with a cheery greeting. He shouted for Dora when he heard Rex's voice on the line.

"Allo!" Dora answered, laying on her fake French accent.

"Hi old girl. You'll never guess what I've got in my hand."

Dora squealed, playing her role to the hilt. "You got the invitation?"

"I did, indeed. However, I wanted to let you know I'll be a few minutes late picking you up."

"Oh?" Dora's voice was laced with concern.

"Nothing to worry about. I've got a letter in hand to drop by Lord Audley's on my way back into town."

"I see..." Dora's tone shifted from concerned to curious. "Are you still going to have a peek around at the castle before you come back?"

"Yes," Rex answered, glancing again at the letter in his hand. "I hear the Semi-State room is particularly interesting."

"Room? I thought there were multiple Semi-State rooms? I read about them in a magazine."

Rex's stomach soured. He'd forgotten that the rooms in questions lined a long hallway. "You don't say! I'll have a nosey and see if any particular one strikes my fancy. Until later. Ta, old girl!"

He replaced the handset on the holder. Their informant was still keeping their cards close to the chest. But now that he had a lead, perhaps he'd spot some clue that would narrow the field.

There was only one way to find out.

* * *

Rex found the uniformed warden waiting outside the office door. Today was indeed his lucky day. He'd know that crooked smile and wavy brown hair anywhere. He didn't need to read the name emblazoned on the badge. Sergeant John Smythe was one of his old trench-mates from the war.

Nothing forged a bond like dodging bullets and helping one another fasten a gas mask. Rex was confident he could convince the man to take him anywhere he needed to go.

"Sergeant Smythe, is that you?" he asked in a jolly voice. "I haven't seen you since you boarded the boat in France. Look at you now!"

Smythe wore the traditional red coat and black trousers. He had a bearskin hat tucked under his arm. Although the royal guards were known for their serious demeanour, the man matched Rex's smile with one of his own.

"Captain Bankes-Fernsby! I didn't expect to see you here."

"That's Lord Reginald," the prince's private secretary corrected.

"Rex, to friends... and Smythe here certainly fits the bill. You couldn't have selected a better man to show me around if you'd tried." Rex thanked the secretary again for her help before heading off on his tour of the castle grounds.

Rex and Smythe spent much of their time together catching up on their lives. Although they came from very different walks of life, the war had a way of bridging the gaps. Rather than following the paths of the visiting tourists, Rex asked Smythe to show him the more private areas.

They began by visiting the guards' rooms and mess hall, then wandered through the different towers before taking a moment of silence in St George's Chapel. Eventually, they arrived at the upper ward where the royal family and their guests had their apartments.

"My friend Miss Laurent mentioned reading about the Semi-State rooms in a magazine. I don't suppose you could show me where they're located, particularly in relation to the hall where tonight's event will take place." Rex went on to explain, "This place is so huge, I fear I'll never find them again if I don't first learn the way."

Smythe was quick to agree to the request on one condition. "I've seen your photos in the papers. Will you tell me what she's really like? I'm sure the society columnists exaggerate."

"Oh no, she's all that they say and more," Rex assured him, adding a wink. "You've got yourself a deal."

Rex regaled Smythe with tales of Dora's more notorious incidents. Rex had the guard so distracted that he thought nothing of it when Rex peppered in questions about alternate pathways to reach the corridor in question. It proved one thing to be true — Dora was so scintillating an individual that she didn't even have to be there to tie a man up in knots.

The second time Rex and Smythe arrived at the first of the line of Semi-State rooms, Rex glanced at his watch and apologised to Smythe for keeping him so long. "You can leave me here, old chap. I know how to get to the terrace and from there, the exit to the car park is easy enough to find." Rex clapped Sergeant Smythe on his back and sent him on his way.

Finally, the location of the secret meeting. Rex opened the first doorway to reveal a lavish crimson drawing room. With the sun flooding through the windows, he almost had to cover his eyes against the shine of the gilt painted on every surface. From the walls to the ceiling to the heavy picture frames, gold was the dominant colour in the room, even outmatching the crimson silk wallpaper.

Rex was certain both his grandmother and Dora would approve. It was exactly what one expected to find in a castle.

Unfortunately, there were no signs of anything outside of the ordinary — for the royal's private entertainment chambers, that is. Rex crossed the room and passed through the next doorway. This room maintained the rich theme, but this time choosing blue to offset the gold.

The third room was already occupied.

"Benedict!" Rex exclaimed. He was so caught off guard by the presence of Dora's brother, he spoke before thinking.

"Rex!" Benedict moved away from the antique clock he was admiring and came over to offer Rex a hand. "What are you doing here?"

"I'd ask you the same," Rex replied, buying himself time to come up with an explanation.

"I came with Father and Mother. Queen Mary offered us accommodation for the weekend festivities." Benedict shrugged. "Now that my father has ascended in the political world, we keep finding ourselves in the most unusual places. Are you coming to the party?" Benedict froze. "Alone? Tell me you're coming alone."

Rex gave an apologetic smile. "Do you honestly believe a woman like Theodora would allow a man to leave her at home while he attended a royal engagement party?"

Benedict wiped his hand over his face and groaned in frustration. He didn't need to explain why. The Cavendish family had worked hard over the last few months to avoid having everyone at the same event. Benedict and Dora had few features in common. But if you stood them together with their parents, it would be impossible to miss the family resemblance.

"I'll make sure to tell her to keep an eye out for you," Rex assured him. Rex turned to leave, but spun back around when another question came to mind. "I don't suppose you've seen anyone else come through these rooms?"

"A maid left as I was coming in, and one of the footman asked if I wanted any refreshments."

"Anyone else? Perhaps a guest?"

"None that I've seen," Benedict answered. "The footman mentioned that Lady Elizabeth usually stops by around mid-afternoon. I suspect he told me so I'd make sure to leave before then... to give the woman a bit of privacy."

Rex cocked his head to the side, not following Benedict's train of thought.

"It's one thing for you and me to take a gander at the furnishings. It's another to imagine living here forever. Bertie may be the spare, but Edward shows no signs of settling down. If he and Elizabeth aren't careful, either they or their children could end up shouldering the weight of the crown."

Benedict's words rang in Rex's mind during his drive home.

Chapter 4
A Royal Explanation

D ora smoothed her dress over her hips and then stepped
out from behind the black lacquered screen in the corner
of her Belgravia bedroom. She sauntered past Inga Kay, her best
friend and lifelong companion, before posing with her arms out
at her side. "So? What do you think?"

Inga pulled a face. "I thought you were planning to keep a
low profile."

"I am. That's why I chose dark blue satin."

"What about the yards of lace on the bodice and feathers at
your shoulders? Not to mention how it clings to your curves
when you move." Inga looked skyward, as though searching the
universe for help. Was there no way to make her dearest friend
understand what keeping a low profile meant?

The divine failed to provide an answer, unless one counted
the hiss from Rex's cat. Mews was curled in a ball near the
bedroom fireplace and didn't appreciate Inga's growl of
frustration.

Dora laughed at Inga's difficulty. "There's no need to
despair. I'm not that ridiculous, you know. I started my
shopping trip with every intention of finding something

appropriately sedate. But when has Theodora Laurent ever dressed like a plain Jane? If I showed up at an event dressed like an innocent debutante, tongues would be wagging before I even stepped out of the car."

Inga flattened her lips. "You have a point. I suppose you chose this colour because it was dark enough to blend into the shadows?"

Dora spun around and gave Inga a sly grin over her shoulder. "You know me so well, darling."

"Too well," Inga muttered.

Dora turned a deaf ear to that last remark. She expected that to be the end of the discussion about her choice of clothing. Inga, however, didn't get that memo. When Dora walked off to check her face, Inga followed so closely behind that Dora could smell the spicy scent of her friend's perfume.

Dora glanced over her shoulder, but one look at Inga's stern expression had her skedaddling out of the way.

"How are you going to style your hair? And don't wear those earrings! They're far too simple for the occasion." Inga hurried past Dora and set to work, searching through the velvet-lined, solid-silver jewellery box.

Dora crossed her arms over her chest and surveyed her friend. If there was one word to describe Inga, it was imperturbable. Yet the woman pawed through the necklaces and bracelets with an almost frenetic pace.

This level of concern was entirely unwarranted. This was far from Dora's first mission, or even her hundredth. Dora decided it was time to intervene. She touched Inga's arm to get her attention.

"Is there something I don't know about tonight's event? You were less stressed about my wardrobe choices when I went to the private audience with the pope."

"Well, I'm not Catholic, now am I?" Inga retorted. "But I

am British, as are you. You're going into the home of our sovereigns. Even if you don't subscribe to the divine right of the king, you can hardly deny their place in our society. Or their dedication to the cause of our nation. We owe them respect. After all, they spend their entire lives in service."

"Like we do?" Dora wasn't aiming to start an argument, but this particular conversation struck a nerve. "Or my father? Or Lord Audley? What about the men who fought and died?" She gave a slow shake of her head. "Once you look past the crowns, the royals are just people, Inga."

Inga opened her mouth to retort, but stopped herself. A strange expression crossed her face. "I've never thought about it that way."

Dora studied her friend's face. Both women had been born into the trappings of wealth and raised with all the privileges that came with the proverbial silver spoon. Yet, despite this similarity, their backgrounds included a key difference. Inga's family descended from landed gentry. They'd accumulated wealth, but no titles. Her father and grandfather had earned much of their money through hard work and ingenuity. Their money could open doors, but their involvement in commerce prevented them from accessing the highest social circles.

Dora's family had generations of titles and prestige behind them. Even if they squandered their funds, the Duke and Duchess of Dorset would still retain their place in the upper class. As much as Dora hated to admit it, she'd leveraged their titles more than once to get her way.

It wasn't until she worked as a nurse in the Great War that she'd understood the flip side to the coin. She'd used her privilege to buy her way to the front lines. The cries of the dying men had broken the lens of her proverbial rose-tinted glasses. There, she'd done her best to give back to those whom society deemed as lesser.

But there was no denying that the harsh realities of war had stripped away the last of her childish notions.

"I'm sure you think me jaded, and perhaps even disrespectful of my upbringing. However, I've seen too much of the people at the top and how they act when they think no one is looking. Those memories pale in comparison to the heroic efforts of the common men who fought and died for their country. Can you honestly tell me that political manoeuvres or war glories of some long dead ancestor make one man more worthy than another?"

Inga stilled before giving a solemn nod of understanding. "I've often wondered how you can be so calm when meeting with the men and women whose names will live on in history books. Listening to you now, I begin to understand. You've learned how to see past the pretence."

"Yes, people have to earn my respect the hard way." Dora's harsh expression softened into a gentle smile. "You, Harris, Rex, and Lord Audley, to name a few, are the types of people I hold in the highest regard. I'd even go so far as to say that you have become the standard against which I measure everyone else. It's as much your fault as mine that the kings, presidents, and other leaders of the world fall short in my eyes."

For once, Inga didn't have a smart retort.

Dora perched on her dressing table stool and gave her makeup a last check. She dusted powder across her nose, taking care to keep any from spilling on her dress. Inga passed her earrings, a necklace, and bracelet, watching as Dora donned the accessories.

The pair stared at Dora's reflection in the mirror. From the quality of her designer gown to the perfect feather adorning her headband, Dora was the picture of entitlement. The oval sapphires winking from her ears and around her neck completed the look.

Dora sighed and then reached up and patted the hand Inga had rested on her shoulder. "Will it make you feel better if I confess that I hold Bertie in admiration?"

Inga's eyebrows shot up. "That's unexpected. Why?"

"For you to understand, I need to tell you about the first time I spoke to him."

"When was that? I assume it must have been in your younger years."

"It was at one of the annual Easter parties at the king's estate in Sandringham. That particular year, my mother dressed me up in a pale green dress covered in yards of Belgian lace and decorated with satin ribbons. She threatened dire consequences if I did anything to mess it up. Worse yet, she told my brothers they'd suffer the same if they did anything to encourage me to misbehave.

"Thus, my brothers refused to even consider allowing me to play with them, consigning me to the group seated on the terrace. The girls my age were boring — only interested in playacting like little ladies. They spent the party prattling on about fashion and future husbands."

"You're happy enough to talk about both of those things now," Inga pointed out with a snort of laughter.

"Yes, but now I'm an adult. At the tender age of nine, I thought boys were gross – albeit in a fun way – and dresses were restrictive."

Inga held up a hand to stop Dora's excuses. "We're getting off track. What about Bertie?"

"I was just getting to that. When the butler announced it was time for the Easter egg hunt, I took the opportunity to sneak off. I went to the library, fully expecting to find it empty. However, Bertie had beaten me there. He was curled up in a window seat, reading a book. He stuttered out a hello when I came in and then blushed in embarrassment."

"I'd forgotten that about him," Inga said, adding, "that he has a stutter. That would make any childhood challenging, but even more so if you had to grow up in the public eye."

Dora nodded in agreement. "When it became clear that I'd come to the library for the same reason as he had, he invited me to pick a book and stay to read with him. He even asked a footman to bring us punch and a plate of iced biscuits." Dora's voice trailed off as she lost herself in her recollections.

After a moment, Inga cleared her throat. "That's a lovely story, but usually, people have to work much harder to gain your admiration."

Dora flashed a wry grin. "Do you know, I almost wish the story ended there? While we were waiting on the food and drink to arrive, Bertie suggested I check out his fiction collection, located on a bottom shelf behind a large wingback. Blocked from view, when I heard the door open, I assumed it was the footman with the tray of nibbles. Then a man's voice boomed, echoing off the hard wooden surfaces of the library shelves. I froze in place.

"It was the king. He roared at Bertie, taking him to task for hiding from their guests. He said Bertie didn't understand the first thing about duty and responsibility. I had never heard an adult speak to a child that way. In a word, it was terrifying."

"So... you pity Bertie?" Inga asked.

"At first, but then my emotions went in a different direction. At any point in time during his father's wrath, Bertie could have pointed out that I was there as well. He could have pulled me into the firing line and used me as a defence. But instead, he took the verbal flogging and followed the king back out to the party, leaving me to escape with none the wiser."

That was enough to raise Bertie in Dora's estimation. It wasn't easy living in such a household. Prince Edward was the golden son. The king had cast Bertie as a failure. His choices had repercussions.

Edward's reckless nature and Bertie's introverted tendencies were no surprise to her, having seen them as children. She wondered whether the king recognised his role in the formation of their personalities.

She doubted it. That was why she avoided events where the king and queen were likely to make an appearance. Dora had learned the hard way about the downside of meeting a hero.

She met Inga's gaze in the mirror's reflection. "As Gustave Flaubert wrote, *Il ne faut pas toucher aux idoles: la dorure en reste aux mains.*"

"Flaubert? My French is rusty. Can you say it again in plain English?" Inga asked.

"*Don't touch your idols: the gilding will stick to your fingers.*" Dora rubbed her fingers together to emphasise her point. "Our nation's history has as many tales of great leaders as it does of those rulers who enriched themselves at the cost of everyone else. My instincts tell me Bertie would fall into the first group, should he ever get the chance. For now, however, he's stuck living in both his father's and brother's shadows."

Lord Audley hadn't needed to ask Dora to take on this mission. As soon as she had heard that it was Bertie who was being threatened, she'd been happy to rush to his aid. It didn't matter that Bertie would not connect her to the young girl he'd saved from his father's wrath. She would know. That was enough.

"Thank you for telling me the story," Inga said. "You have a knack for making me view the world through a different lens. I'm glad that you and Rex will be the ones keeping watch over Prince Bertie and his future bride."

"Do me a favour and keep your fingers and toes crossed that the situation will resolve this evening."

Despite extracting a promise from Inga to think only good thoughts, Dora struggled to hold on to her hope for a positive outcome. The clock hanging over her head continued to count down the minutes until their midnight meeting. Dora felt sure they'd done all they could. But would it be enough?

She consoled herself as best as she could. If their plans went awry, their anonymous informant would simply fail to turn up. As far as worst-case scenarios went, this one hardly ranked in the charts.

Chapter 5
The Fallout

B ACK AT THE SCENE OF THE CRIME
"Drop the knife," Prince Bertie commanded a second time.

Clark unclenched his fist, and the dagger fell to the floor. It landed on the thick, red Aubusson carpet with barely a thud. Nonetheless, the noise made everyone in the room flinch.

Rex took in the sight and suddenly found himself remembering the battlefield. He'd never forget seeing blood spray from Lucien's body as he sacrificed himself to German soldiers so Rex could escape a trap. He saw the trenches and smelled that long-ago war's mud...blood...smoke...and gas.

Death was here, but he was there.

With an act of the will, he inhaled deeply, fighting for calm. The lemon scent of furniture oil fought with the smoke from the open fireplace for dominance. It overcame the smell of blood. He took a second shallower breath, this time through his mouth, and steeled himself to suppress the memories and survivor's guilt.

He leaned closer to Dora, letting her floral-scented perfume pull him back to the present. Although their mission had now gone horribly awry, he had no choice but to see this night through...and he would.

On steadier ground, Rex chanced a look at Prince Bertie and Thomas Liddell. Like him, the men seemed to be holding their own against the terrible circumstances. Bertie's hands were balled into tight fists at his side, while Thomas glared daggers at Clark.

This was, without a doubt, fast becoming one of the worst nights of Rex's post-war life. Yet, he was sure it paled in comparison to how Clark felt. Clark had a wild-eyed look on his face, and swayed perilously close to the chair occupied by the victim.

"Sit down," Rex ordered him.

Thomas Liddell turned his heated glare in Rex's direction.

"It does us no good if he faints atop the body," Rex added, pointing Clark toward the nearest empty couch. Upholstered in rose velvet, with ornate gold legs and arms, Rex half-feared the antique might collapse under Clark's weight. Fortunately, it was studier than it looked.

Now that he'd resolved the immediate threat of danger, Rex glanced at the woman at his side. Dora's strawberry blonde hair glowed like pure spun gold against the gilded room. She handled herself with aplomb, carefully schooling her expression.

Dora gazed back and gave the slightest inclination of her head. Without needing to say a word, they knew what they had to do.

Rex and Dora moved in different directions. Dora hurried over to comfort Prince Bertie, leaving Rex to deal with Clark.

Rex took a moment to get his bearings. The dead man sat, half-slumped in a wingback chair, with his arm dangling over the armrest. Rex didn't have a clear view of the man's face. The man wore the traditional black coat and tails. His sleeve had pulled up enough to reveal a jewelled cufflink. All this confirmed the man must have been a guest, but did little more than that. Even his hair, a muddy brown colour, failed to offer any hint as to his identity.

Given there were no signs of life, Rex focused his attention on the only person he could help.

One of his closest friends in the world - Lord Clark Kenworthy.

Rex's long legs ate up the space as he crossed the room to where his friend sat.

Clark hardly made note of Rex's arrival. He was too busy staring at his stained glove and mumbling under his breath. "The blood was dripping. I thought... I was trying to help him. The dagger slid out... But it was stupid of me. He was already dead." He raised his head then and met Rex's eyes. "I never should have touched it."

Rex settled gently beside Clark. He lifted his hand and patted Clark's back the way a mother would comfort a crying child. The strange juxtaposition of the bloodstain and the red furnishings lent the moment a sense of surreality.

While Clark got a hold of himself, Rex shifted around until he saw the face of the dead man.

It was Lord Hugh FitzClarence. His hooked nose dominated his slack features and helped Rex identify him. Although he'd been only a year ahead of Rex in school, Rex barely knew him.

That didn't stop Rex's mind from filling with a list of questions.

Was this their anonymous informant? Or was Hugh the one making the threats? Whatever his involvement, he'd had taken it to his grave.

Hugh was slumped awkwardly in the seat, leaving Rex with the impression that he had not been seated when he was stabbed. If Rex had to guess, the man had been standing, facing his murderer, when the dagger struck home. Hugh must have stumbled back and landed in the chair. Based on the bloodstain on the right side of his chest, the dagger had slid between his ribs and directly into his heart.

He'd never had a chance.

Rex forced his gaze away at the sound of approaching footsteps. It was the prince, accompanied by Dora. Bertie's eyes grew wide. He looked at the victim's face, and his mouth dropped open in a rictus of horror as reality set in. His best friend was dead, murdered in a supposed stronghold, on the night of Bertie's engagement party.

Dora laid her fingers on the prince's arm to pull his attention away. "Maybe you should sit too..."

Prince Bertie declined her suggestion. "As much as I hate it, this is hardly the first time I've had a brush with death. This isn't even the first time the dead is someone I called a friend."

His words held true for all of them. Having served in the Great War, they each had far too much experience with loss.

Bertie forced himself to turn his back on Hugh. There was nothing he could do for him now. It was to Clark that he posed his questions. "Why are you here?"

Clark drew a steadying breath. Before he could answer, Thomas Liddell joined the rest of them on their side of the room. They formed a semicircle around Clark. Rex sat at his side, Dora and Bertie stood across from him, and Thomas blocked the way between Clark and the door. He made it clear Clark wasn't going anywhere without a full explanation.

"I had a note," Clark said. He reached up with his right hand before remembering the blood on his glove. After a moment of awkward silence, he used his left hand to pull a crumpled piece of paper from his coat pocket. He unfolded it, revealing a short, handwritten line inside, and held it out to Rex. "You told me to come, not ten minutes ago."

Rex rocked back and scrunched his brow. "I didn't send you any note. I couldn't have. Ten minutes ago, I was dancing with Theodora."

Thomas grabbed the paper from Clark's hand and looked down at it. "He's right, Lord Rex. It's signed in your name."

Dora shuffled closer and peered at the paper. "Let me see."

Thomas refused to let go, but unbent enough to hold up the slip of paper so she could see it better.

"That isn't Rex's handwriting. I should know, given the number of love notes he's penned."

Thomas shrugged off her statement. "Lord Clark obviously forged this, in case he was caught. The evidence of his involvement is still dripping from his hand. No one move. I'm going for the guards." Thomas didn't wait for anyone else to agree. He spun around and marched out of the room, closing the door firmly behind him.

"You'll have to excuse him," Bertie explained, motioning toward the closed door. "Hugh was his brother-in-law."

"And your friend, non?" Dora asked, layering on her adopted French accent. "I've seen him with you at other events, but I didn't know his name."

She obviously knew as well as him the identity of the dead man. But when Prince Bertie began telling her more about Hugh, he understood why she'd pretended otherwise.

"His name is Hugh FitzClarence. We've been friends for years. Thomas, as well. We were all at Eton. It was Thomas, in fact, who helped arrange the marriage between Hugh and his sister Tabitha." Prince Bertie rubbed his forehead. "What are we going to tell Tabitha?"

"Should we send someone to fetch her?" Dora asked.

"No, she shouldn't see him like this. It will be hard enough

to hear, without having the evidence in front of her face."
Thomas returned just then, accompanied by Lord Nicholas van
Solms, another member of Prince Bertie's inner circle.

Although Nicholas must have been told what to expect, he
still lurched sideways when they caught sight of Hugh's body.
He ran his fingers through his auburn hair and murmured in
dismay. Based on his dishevelled state, this wasn't the first time
he'd done so.

A trio of armed guards followed Thomas and Nicholas into
the state room where the rest had remained.

Thomas didn't waste any time. Without asking anyone's
leave, he pointed a finger in Clark's direction. "Take that man
into custody."

The guards didn't move. Instead, they looked to their prince
for permission. Bertie's conflicted expression held them at bay.

While they were content to wait, Thomas was not. "Bertie,
you can't mean to let him go! Not considering we discovered
him with the weapon in hand! Lock him up and toss away the
key."

Clark's face grew paler, a feat Rex would have deemed
impossible before now. "I didn't do it," he spluttered. "You have
to believe me! Find the footman who gave me the note. He can
attest to my innocence."

Rex could feel the situation slipping into chaos. He had to
act fast if he was going to retain any semblance of control over
what happened next. Whatever he did, he couldn't let the
guards drag his best friend away. Rex didn't need to speak with
any footman to know Clark to be innocent.

He held out his hands and appealed for calm. "Right now,
we are the only people who know Hugh is dead. If the guards
drag Clark from this room, and the police show up en masse,
what do you think will be the result?"

"He's right," Nicholas said, voicing his agreement. He

stopped tugging on his hair long enough to add an explanation. "I can already imagine the headlines in the papers. *Lord Hugh Dead! Engagement cursed!* This cannot leak into the public domain."

Bertie struggled to get a word out, his stutter growing worse under the stress. Finally, he said, "I had a hard enough time convincing Elizabeth to accept my proposal. This might scare her away from the altar."

Thomas swung around, hardly able to believe his ears. "What of Hugh's bride? What am I meant to tell Tabitha when she asks where he is? She's my sister, for god's sake!"

Rex feared the two friends would come to blows if someone didn't act fast.

Nicholas recognised the risk as well. "I may have a solution."

Thomas's face remained flushed with anger, but he took a half-step backwards, giving Nicholas room to speak.

"Rupert has a connection at Scotland Yard. A Detective Chief Inspector there, well placed, as far as I know. Served in the trenches with Rupert. He was kind enough to help us when we got into a spot of trouble a couple of years ago."

"Who is Rupert?" Dora asked, once again feigning ignorance.

Prince Bertie was the one to answer. "There are only a handful of people I trust implicitly. Nicholas and Thomas are here. Rupert is the third. Nicholas, track him down and explain. You'll need a phone." Bertie looked at the guards. "One of you escort them to the nearest private line, please."

"What of the rest of us?" Rex asked.

Bertie wiped his hand over his mouth, his heartfelt pain writ across his classic features. "We will have the hardest part of all. We must return to the celebration, before anyone remarks on our absence. Thomas, I suggest you find a way to extract your sister and let her know the news. You can use my quarters."

Thomas's nostrils flared, but he didn't argue. "Fine, but he stays here."

The *he* in question was obviously Clark.

"I'll stay with him, and the guard can remain, too," Dora said, speaking up. "If anyone misses me, Rex can tell them I've gone to powder my nose."

"Is that acceptable?" Bertie asked Thomas.

"Yes, but only if they sit at the other end of the room. I won't take any chances that the two of them might mess with the evidence."

Rex bit back a retort. Now wasn't the time to stand up for Dora's and Clark's reputations.

Clark rose without a word and followed Dora as she guided him to the far side of the room. If anything, he seemed relieved to get some distance from the body.

Rex followed Prince Bertie and Thomas out of the room, taking one last glance before he closed the door, leaving Dora and Clark behind.

Dora was already busy helping Clark remove the offensive glove from his hand. Another woman would have swooned at the thought, but Dora was made of sterner stuff.

Thank goodness for that. The dead man, threats against the prince, and Clark's freedom left Rex and Dora with no time to worry about sensibilities.

Chapter 6
Scotland Yard's Best

Dora watched as Clark took a sip of his whiskey. His hand no longer trembled where he held the glass. If it weren't for the lines creasing his forehead, she'd almost believe that her attempts at distracting him were having some effect.

Left behind while the other men returned to the celebration, Dora had concentrated her efforts on keeping Clark's spirits up. She'd recounted story after story of her adventures. However, even her most bizarre adventures couldn't compare with the sword of Damocles, that was dangling by a thin thread over Clark's neck.

Despite her promises that everything would work out as it should in the end, Clark was clearly still terrified. Anyone would be in his shoes. Dora had to admit that even she might falter in his position.

Clark's gaze strayed toward the silent guard standing watch at the other end of the room. Dressed in the scarlet tunic and black trousers of the Royal Guard, the man was between them and the door. He stood firm, almost daring them to attempt to get past, even though escape was the furthest thing from their minds.

Dora gave a polite cough to pull Clark's attention her way.

"I'm sorry, Dora. I doubly appreciate you remaining behind, given I'm such poor company," Clark said.

Dora brushed the apology aside. "None of this is your fault."

"Well, at least part of it is. If I hadn't laid a hand on that dagger, I doubt we'd be sitting here right now."

Dora nodded her head in agreement, even though she knew that wasn't true. No matter what, she'd have been in this room.

Clark reached over and grasped Dora's hand. He gave it a squeeze while raising his gaze until it met hers. "I don't know how I will ever repay you for your fortitude. Anyone else would have hesitated to leap to my defence after finding me as you did. It means so much to me that you and Rex both believed me innocent."

"As if we'd do otherwise!" Dora replied without an ounce of hesitation. "When Rex was in dire straits at Ducklington Manor, you not only pledged to help, but provided the final clue we needed to solve the mystery. Think of it as us returning the favour. You are guilty of many things, Clark, but murder isn't one of them."

Some of the tension in Clark's shoulders eased. But his relief didn't last long. "You saw the look on Thomas's face. He isn't going to let this drop. He'll see me hanged if he can."

Dora held tighter to Clark's hand and squeezed it back. "Don't despair," she begged. "The detective from Scotland Yard will take control when he arrives. He won't be emotionally involved. I'm confident he'll quickly see the folly of pursuing you as a suspect."

As if conjured by her words, the door to the Crimson Semi-State room opened and an unfamiliar man came in. Dora sized him up in a matter of seconds. Instead of black tie, the man wore a suit. The fabric of the coat wasn't the cheapest, but the suit showed signs of wear at the elbows and the trousers were a smidgen too large. Dora didn't need to see a warrant card to know that this was the detective.

A group of men followed on his heels. Prince Bertie led the pack, with Lord Rupert and Rex entering one after the other, and Lord Audley closing the door behind them.

Dora was hardly surprised to see Audley join the group, but Clark was caught off guard. "Prince Bertie likely asked Lord Audley to join," she whispered. "I saw them speaking earlier."

The guard moved aside, clearing the way for the men to move to the middle of the room.

Bertie took charge of the introductions. "Lord Clark, Miss Laurent, this is Detective Chief Inspector Jonathan Miller of Scotland Yard."

Miller nodded at them both, but his expression didn't reveal any clue as to his thoughts. He went over to get a better look at the body, standing silently for a few moments while he took in the scene. Given the lack of further clues, he had little choice but to move straight on to questions.

"Is there another room we can use?" he asked Bertie.

"The Blue Room next door is empty. We can go in there."

Miller instructed the guard to remain at his post and then followed the rest.

As with the Crimson Room, the Blue Room took its name from its to decor. The silk-covered walls were painted robin's egg blue, and the couches upholstered in royal blue velvet. Golden gilt shined from the wooden surfaces, where a designer had applied it with a heavy hand. An extravagant blue and gold Aubusson carpet pulled the room together.

Clusters of chairs and fainting couches dotted the length of the room, providing intimate seating areas. Bertie strode toward a larger grouping of furniture at the far end of the room. With two couches and several chairs, there was space enough for everyone.

Dora guided Clark to a large couch upholstered in blue silk and cotton damask and sat beside him. Rex chose the remaining seat, allowing the two of them to effectively flank Clark in a show of moral support.

Bertie and Rupert claimed a pair of matching cherry wood Chippendale chairs. Lord Audley did not sit, instead choosing to stand behind Prince Bertie's chair. As ever, he was the man behind the throne.

DCI Miller sat on the smaller, matching two-seater couch opposite Clark. He unbuttoned his jacket and pulled a notepad and pen from the inside pocket. He crossed his legs, resting his foot upon his knee, and settled back to begin his questioning.

While DCI Miller gathered his thoughts, Dora studied Rupert. He was short of stature and barrel chested. He walked with a limp, testament to his time spent at the front. Both he and Bertie displayed a remarkable calm, despite the obviously stressful and unhappy circumstances in which they found themselves.

DCI Miller tapped his pen on his paper to get their attention and then posed his first question. "Let's start at the beginning. Which one of you was the first to arrive?"

All eyes turned to Clark. Clark's face drained of colour, and he gulped. "Yes, I arrived before everyone else, but only because I received a message asking me to come. Hugh was already dead, and whoever killed him, long gone."

Miller made a note. "What of the rest of you? I understand several of you were on hand to discover Lord Clark standing over the body. What led you to be here?"

Dora and Rex remained absolutely silent. Prince Bertie shifted in his seat to glance over his shoulder at Lord Audley.

Lord Audley took that as his cue to step in. "I received a request from someone who wanted a private audience with Prince Albert, and I passed it along at the requested time."

Miller waited a moment, but when Lord Audley failed to add further explanation, he was forced to ask. "Who requested the audience?"

Dora was curious to see what Lord Audley would say. She had no idea whether he'd spoken with Bertie in the interim, nor what he felt comfortable revealing to the detective.

Lord Audley wiped his hand across the back of his neck, looking pained as he admitted, "I don't know. All I can confirm is that the person was already on the guest list for tonight's celebration. I had no reason to fear for Prince Albert's safety, nor for anyone else."

Prince Bertie picked up the thread. "Don't give him too hard a time. People are always leveraging their connections to have a word with me, my brother, or father. The only unusual aspect was that they wanted to speak to me tonight. After Lord Audley passed along the message, I excused myself from the celebration and ventured to the Crimson Room for the meeting. I ran into Thomas, Thomas Liddell, that is, on my way. Lord Rex and Miss Laurent must have been close enough to hear our gasps."

DCI Miller turned his gaze on Dora and Rex and arched an eyebrow.

Lord Audley coughed politely. "I asked Lord Rex to keep an eye on Prince Albert. He did it as a favour for me."

"I thought you said you had no fear, yet you sent another guest along? Why didn't you tell the guards to accompany the prince?" Miller asked.

"I was curious to see who dared to make demands of me. Lord Rex served under my command during the war, and I knew him capable of dealing with tricky situations that require discretion. If anything went wrong, I trusted Lord Rex would go for help. But again, I stress, I didn't expect the situation to warrant it."

Miller held Audley's gaze, as if he were searching his

expression for some hidden information. However, Audley was a master at keeping secrets. Miller would find no inspiration there.

Dora held back a smile when Miller was the first to blink.

He lowered his gaze to the pad in his hand and added all of this to his notes. He then raised his head and surveyed the room. "So? Was our victim the person who requested the meeting?"

All around the room he was met with shaking heads, Prince Bertie the most emphatic.

"Hugh was one of my closest friends. We've known each other for years. There is no reason for him to approach a third party to ask for my time. He knew my door was always open to him."

DCI Miller pondered Bertie's answer in light of the situation. "I beg your pardon, your highness, but might I speak plainly?"

"Of course."

"Given you know him so well, why is he dead? Who do you think killed him?"

"To this, I cannot offer an answer. Despite having found Lord Clark in a compromising position, I don't know of any reason why he would want Hugh dead. The entire situation is confounding."

Dora was surprised by Prince Bertie's willingness to offer Clark a helping hand. In his position, she wasn't sure she would be so quick or capable of keeping an open mind. DCI Miller also seemed to be impressed by the prince, but he gave no sign of excluding Clark from the suspect list.

"When was Hugh last seen alive?"

The members of the group took a moment to compare their recollections. Given the size of the event, they'd each seen Hugh at varying points in time. In the end, they agreed it had been at least a half hour before they found his body that anyone remembered seeing him.

"Perhaps Hugh's wife will be better able to respond." Rupert said, finally speaking up. "She is currently upstairs, in Bertie's private quarters, with her brother Thomas. We thought it best to escort her away from the event before she asked questions none of us were ready to answer."

"Thomas? The same Thomas who was walking with you when you arrived here, your highness?" Miller asked the prince.

"Yes."

DCI Miller was clearly intrigued by this response.

Noting his curious expression, Rupert rushed to explain the connections. "Hugh, Thomas, Nicholas, and I are all close friends with Prince Bertie. There was nothing unusual about any of us being together."

DCI Miller flicked a glance at Clark. "I note your name wasn't included. Since you are the odd man out, do you have any guess why you ended up involved?"

"I wish I weren't," Clark exclaimed in frustration. "A footman passed me a note telling me to come here. It was signed with Lord Rex's name, but he says it wasn't from him. I didn't notice at the time, but he's right. The handwriting is off."

At this, Prince Bertie pulled the note from his pocket and handed it over to the detective.

The detective tucked the note into the back of his pad. "Is there anything else I should know? No matter how small, if you believe it might be relevant, now is the time to say it." DCI Miller shifted his gaze from person to person, lingering long enough to give them time to speak up.

The only answer he got was silence.

Everyone watched to see what DCI Miller would say next. The time and place required a delicate hand, but given that someone had been murdered, Miller must have known that he couldn't leave things there. The questions of why Hugh had been in that room, and who'd slipped a dagger between his ribs, had to be answered.

After a long pause, DCI Miller shared his thoughts. "You have asked me to handle this with kid gloves, and so I shall. Although I don't like it, I understand the ramifications of this getting out. If we were anywhere else, under any other circumstances, I'd keep Lord Clark under remand until his innocence could be proven. However, I recognise that doing so would raise eyebrows, perhaps ones the royal family would prefer remain unmoved. What would you have me do?"

Lord Audley must have prepared for this moment, as he was quick to reply. "Might I offer a suggestion? I often play the role of problem-solver for the royal family. What if you were to remand Lord Clark into my care? This would keep word from getting out and also ensure Lord Clark doesn't run off — not that I have any fear of this. It is in all our interest to stick as close as we can to the letter of the law."

DCI Miller inclined his head, appearing to agree, but he waited until Prince Bertie gave his approval.

Clark heaved a sigh of relief. Although this wasn't his ideal outcome, it was certainly much better than the alternatives.

Audley moved out from behind the chair and motioned for Clark to stand. "Very well, if the castle can spare a guard, I'd ask them to escort Clark to his home so he can gather what he needs, and then deliver him to my mansion in Mayfair."

Dora tugged on Clark's trousers before he walked away. When he turned around, she whispered, "We'll call on you tomorrow. I promise."

Rex was close enough to hear her words and added a quiet agreement.

There was nothing more any of them could do. Miller took control of the crime scene and sent everyone back to finish out their night as though all was normal. Dora hoped that Bertie and Rupert were up to the task of feigning a celebratory mood despite the loss of their dear friend.

As for her and Rex, they too would have to set aside their personal concerns. When duty called, there was no space for emotions.

As they left the room, Dora kept a close eye on Lord Audley, looking to him for the next set of orders. He caught her eye, pushed up his sleeve, and checked his watch.

Dora knew what that meant. Their already long night was nowhere close to an end. As soon as they could leave the castle without attracting undue attention, they were expected for a late night rendezvous with Lord Audley.

Chapter 7
The New Mission

Rex waited in the Grand Vestibule of Windsor Castle. Dora had sworn she'd only be a moment, explaining she needed to powder her nose before they left back for London. Rex had pulled on his winter coat in preparation for heading out into the chilly night air, but Dora had left him long enough that he was beginning to sweat. He turned around at the sound of footsteps approaching, sure it would be her, but found her brother instead.

Lord Benedict Cavendish was a man on a mission. He held Rex's gaze as he approached, practically daring him to attempt to run away.

But Rex knew better. He stood his ground and waited for Benedict to speak his mind.

Benedict, however, didn't intend for others to overhear their conversation. Instead, he asked the footman standing silently in the corner if there was a room they could use for a private conversation. The footman pointed them towards the nearest antechamber. Benedict strode inside, assuming Rex would follow. He did, but only after telling the footman to keep an eye out for Dora.

Rex closed the door behind himself. The room they were in was small by Windsor standards. The furnishings were sparse: a pair of wingback chairs, a large rug, and a single floor lamp lighting the room. If it weren't for the obligatory gold gilt, one could be in any great house.

Benedict spoke. "What happened?"

Rex feigned a nonchalance he certainly didn't feel. "I have no idea what you mean. It's growing late and Dora and I have a long drive ahead of us. We're on our way out."

Benedict crossed his arms and leaned against the back of a chair. "Don't try to fob me off, Rex. First, I ran into you wandering around earlier today. Then I spotted Harris masquerading as a footman. Ever since then, I've been watching you and Dora like a hawk. I saw Lord Audley whispering in Prince Bertie's ear, and the two of you sneaking off. Bertie's closest friends have come and gone, disappearing without any explanation. Something is afoot."

Rex made a face. He didn't know what he could and could not say. The last thing he wanted to do was tell an outright lie to Dora's brother. After all, they'd worked so hard to foster a good relationship with him.

Fortunately, the scrape of the door opening offered Rex a solution. Dora swept in, hardly raising an eyebrow at finding Rex holed up with her brother.

"I was beginning to think you'd left without me until the footman finally deigned to tell me where you'd gone. Now, as much as I enjoy a cosy conversation, the hour is late. If you two are finished, can we go?"

Benedict did not move. His studious gaze skimmed the pair of lovebirds, searching them for clues. "You expect me to believe that the notorious night owls are leaving early? If you don't give me some hint as to what has happened, I'll go to Bertie instead."

As far as threats went, that one was particularly effective. Rex looked at Dora. "He saw Harris."

Dora was capable of explaining many things, but why her butler was in Windsor Castle wasn't one of them. She shrugged. There was nothing for it but to come clean. After all, Benedict would find out what happened soon enough.

Rex decided to tell him the bare minimum, for now anyway. "Lord Hugh FitzClarence is dead. Prince Bertie made the discovery. We were close enough behind to stumble across the scene."

"Natural causes?" Benedict pursed his lips. "Of course not. Never is with you two. I suppose you are tasked with finding the killer."

"Bertie found Clark standing over the body."

If Rex thought he was going to get away after that bombshell, he was sadly mistaken. Benedict peppered the pair with more questions, but they offered no answers. What could they say? For all they knew, anyone could be listening on the other side of the door.

Eventually, Benedict wound to a stop. "Well, what are you two going to do about it?"

Again, Dora and Rex remained silent.

Benedict scoffed. "Surely you're going to investigate."

"There is already an investigator from Scotland Yard on the case. We'll do all we can to help Clark, within our limitations." Dora allowed a hint of her frustration to show on her face.

"You can count on me to do the same." Benedict let them go after that statement. He extracted a promise that they would keep him as updated as they could, and then they all went their separate ways.

Rex kept Dora close to his side while they waited for the car to be brought around. Between the guards and the other departing guests, there were too many eyes monitoring their every move. They were far from the days of war, yet Rex felt the familiar itch on the back of his neck that came from straying too close to no-man's-land. Someone had them all in their sights. But who?

Dora traced a finger down his arm, pulling him back to the present. "If there is one thing I can say, it is that life with you is never dull. Thank you for arranging for us to attend."

The older matron behind them sniffed with disdain. Rex bit back a chuckle. If he spent any more time with Dora, he'd end up banned from half of London's households. Perhaps that wasn't a bad thing.

He pulled her close. "How could any place be boring when I have you on my arm? Come now, that is our car."

Dora allowed Rex to claim the driver's seat. He made sure she was warm, draping a thick driving blanket over her legs before pulling away from the castle entrance. The Windsor streets required his full attention, so it wasn't until the town was in their rearview mirror that they picked up their conversation.

Given the late hour, there were few cars on the road. Both Rex and Dora were completely sober, having only feigned drinking while at the event. They'd both wanted to keep their wits about them, and thank goodness they had. As it stood, they'd need all their focus to keep track of the lies they told to Prince Bertie and his cohort, DCI Miller, and Benedict.

"Do you think we should have said more to Benedict?" Rex asked, glancing sideways at where Dora sat in the passenger seat.

"Given the location of our conversation, we said probably more than we should have. There's time enough tomorrow to speak with him again. I don't know about you, but I'm exhausted. This is a rare occasion on which I'm actually relieved to have an early night."

"Our night is far from done," Rex reminded Dora. "Would

you prefer to go straight to Lord Audley's house, or first change into something more comfortable at home?"

Dora arched an eyebrow at his question and gave Rex a come-hither look. He wagged a finger at her, and she fluttered her lashes, feigning innocence.

That was how it was between them now. Rex spent more nights at her home than away. Sometimes, lying beside her in the darkness, he felt a twinge of guilt. He'd marry her in a heartbeat if he could.

Although Dora had said many times that she was equally committed to him, for the good of the country, she had to retain her independence.

She'd explained to him, "Theodora Laurent isn't a person. She is an ideal. Marriage would humanise her to a degree we cannot afford."

He was left to answer the question. Which was more important to him, having a relationship recognised by all of society, or living with her, however he could? It had taken him no time at all to arrive at an answer. He was hers, for as long as she'd have him.

Dora's mind must have gone in a similar direction. She slid across the seat and snuggled against him. With the driving rug snug across her lap and the silk-lined cape covering her shoulders, only her face and golden hair were visible. Rex barely resisted the urge to lean over and kiss her. The late-night London traffic required his full attention.

They arrived at Lord Audley's as the nearest church tower chimed three times. The streets of Mayfair were silent in the early morning hour. As dawn approached, the streets would fill with delivery workers bringing food and supplies to the wealthy homes. But now, there was no one to witness them entering Lord Audley's garden. In silence, they crept along the stone pathway leading to the study where he awaited them.

Like them, Lord Audley was still wearing his formal suit. Only the loose bowtie around his neck gave proof to the hour. He told them to leave their coats and hats on a nearby chair and offered them a warm drink laced with brandy. After assuring them Clark was comfortably settled in an upstairs guest room, he wasted no time turning the conversation to their original mission.

"Hugh FitzClarence is dead. Do either of you believe he was the anonymous sender?"

"No," they said in unison. Dora motioned for Rex to go ahead.

"Prince Bertie's and Rupert's explanations of their friendship hold water. It doesn't make sense that he would come to you for help. Or, if he did, he wouldn't do it anonymously."

Lord Audley nodded his agreement. "Then that begs the next question. Is Hugh the person who was plotting against the Prince?"

This time, Dora and Rex didn't have a ready answer.

"He fits the description, but so do all the rest of Bertie's close friends. We have so little to go on, I don't feel comfortable making any assumptions. What would be his motive?" Rex asked.

"That will take time to uncover," Dora answered. "Learning more about Lord Hugh will be our first priority come daybreak."

"I'd like to add another consideration to your list." Audley took a sip of his drink. "What if everything happened exactly as our mystery sender intended? What if they wanted Bertie to discover Hugh's body?"

Rex scowled. With every fibre of his being, he longed to say no, that such a thought was ridiculous. But was it? It wasn't a far slide to go from anonymous notes to secret meetings to staged murders. But in Windsor Castle? If that were the case, their killer was brazen, to say the least.

"That is a very good question," Dora agreed. "But we'd be fools to make guesses. You know what Sherlock Holmes had to say about such situations.

'It is a capital mistake to theorise before one has data. Insensibly one begins to twist facts to suit theories, instead of theories to suit facts.'

"Data is the one thing we are lacking. Our next steps hinge on learning more about Lord Hugh."

"Where do you want to start?" Rex asked.

"With the person who should know him best - his wife. I'll pay a condolence call tomorrow. Even if she is turning away guests, I believe she'll accept me, given we were there when he was found."

"It's a good plan," Audley said. "Report back as soon as you have more information to hand."

Chapter 8
Tea with a Duchess

The Rolls-Royce Phantom prowled through the streets of London, attracting attention wherever it went. Some would say it was the ostentatious car catching everyone's eye. They'd be wrong. Instead, the street vendors, ladies who lunch, and even the busy businessmen all leaned sideways to catch a glimpse of the bejewelled and bedazzling woman riding in the rear seat.

Getting invited into the FitzClarence home would not be easy. Dora was prepared to weaponise every tool at her disposal. Her looks, her wealth, and her connection to one of London's most prestigious families... Rex's that is. No one knew about her own.

Archie pulled to a stop outside of the front gate of an expansive Mayfair home. The white stone facade was cold and unwelcoming. The drawn drapes and darkened windows matched the sombre air of the barren flower beds. It wasn't just the mourning period happening inside. Either you were haughty enough to be undaunted, or you weren't meant to make it past the front gate.

Dora fitted into the first category, whether the home

occupants were willing to agree or not. Archie, however, didn't dare to even approach the gate. He tugged his cap lower and met Dora's eyes in the rearview mirror.

"Want me to wait here in case they turn you away?"

"Absolutely not!" Dora tsked her finger. "Park one street over, and make sure you are out of sight of the doorstep. I don't want to make it easy for them to refuse my entry. Now, be a proper chauffeur and come open this door."

"Yes, madam," Archie stepped out of the car, smoothed his uniform into place, and then executed his duties flawlessly.

Beneath her priceless Siberian sable coat, Dora wore an exquisite creation direct from Lanvin Modes in Paris. She'd borrowed sapphires from the Dowager Duchess to grace her ears and neck. Every time she shook her reddish gold hair, the sapphires glowed in the winter sun.

Dora reminded herself that she was a queen of her own domain while she made her way up the front steps. The fading purr of the car motor confirmed Archie had done as she'd asked. There was no going back now.

There was no knocker on the front door. It was an old-fashioned way of letting visitors know that the household wasn't accepting guests. Dora didn't let that stop her. She rapped directly on the wooden door with her gloved knuckles. After an almost interminable wait, a snotty butler answered the door.

He was short, squat, and sported a rather impressive comb-over, of which Dora had a prime view thanks to her high heels. He didn't let the height difference slow his attempt to look down his nose at her.

It took all her control not to pull a face. Instead, she matched his upright stance with one of her own. She refused to be cowed.

Her card was already in her hand, ready to be passed over. "I'd like to pay my condolences to Her Grace. In person," she added. She held out the card, but he refused to take it. He'd obviously recognised her, which wasn't a surprise given how often her photo graced the society pages.

"The family is not receiving at this time." His snooty voice practically dripped with disdain, communicating the unspoken portion of his response.

Even if they were accepting visitors, their door would never be open to the likes of her.

Dora widened her stance. Two could play at that game.

"No exceptions? Not even for the woman who was there when Prince Albert stumbled upon the duke's body?" She raised her eyebrows and added her own silent note.

There are plenty of other places willing to accept me. Send me away and my next visit might be to the evening papers.

The butler flared his nostrils. "Wait here."

"Of course. I do love to people watch. Who knows who I'll see... or who might see me?"

The only thing worse than having Theodora Laurent inside the house was having her perched on the doorstep for all to see. The rumourmongers would have a field day.

The butler stepped aside and motioned for her to come in. "You may wait in the drawing room while I see whether Her Grace is up to coming down." He led her across the marble floor, past the grand staircase, and into the nearest receiving room. "Please don't touch anything."

Dora pulled her gloves off and wiggled her fingers at his departing back. She was so confident that Lady FitzClarence would come down that she unbuttoned her fur coat and draped it atop the nearest chair. It was too bad the butler hadn't remained behind. He'd have had an apoplexy at seeing Dora make herself at home.

With little else to keep her entertained, Dora surveyed the room. Someone with a love of the Georgian period had selected the furnishings and antiques. Dora bet that someone was from the older generation — Hugh's mother must still be alive.

Here and there, she spotted evidence of the current Duchess's preferences. In between the Gainsboroughs and Constables hung a Chinese silk painted triptych. In place of pride on a marble column near the window sat a Murano glass vase.

Tabitha FitzClarence was a woman slowly growing comfortable with her place as the woman of the house. In another few years, she'd have the whole house redecorated.

That is, assuming she wasn't asked to leave by whomever would inherit Hugh's title.

The door clicked and Lady Tabitha walked in. Dora remembered seeing her at the ball. She'd been standing near Lady Elizabeth and the other women from the highest levels of the haut ton. It seemed her twin brother Thomas wasn't the only one with royal connection.

Tabitha's silk frock hung loosely over her lithe body. She was naturally graced with the angular curves that were all the rage. Dora's first thought was that she looked remarkably well, given her recent loss.

But then Dora noted the handkerchief peeking from the edge of Tabitha's sleeve. When she crossed the room, the light from the crystal chandelier revealed the bruises under her eyes she'd attempted to cover with make-up.

Dora was no longer so sure how well Tabitha was holding up. She was doing an excellent job of playing the role of the strong female. Time would tell whether she had the strength of the oak, or if she'd bend and break like the willow. Dora had to proceed with caution.

Tabitha asked the butler to arrange for tea before introducing herself properly and inviting Dora to sit. A footman arrived in short order with a full tea trolley. He took up position by the door, likely ordered to do so by the butler. Tabitha, however, wasn't keen to have an audience for this conversation. She sent him off with an order to make sure they weren't disturbed.

Once again, Dora viewed the situation like she would a game board. She and Tabitha were virtual strangers, connected by a single extraordinarily terrible event. Both were well-versed in the machinations of high society. If Dora hoped to learn anything of value, she'd need to keep her wits about her.

"I'm very sorry for your loss, Your Grace. If it is any consolation, it didn't appear that the Duke suffered."

"Thank you. May I ask, how did you come to be in the room at the time?"

"I attended the party with Lord Rex — Lord Reginald Bankes-Fernsby. He was showing me more of the castle."

"Ah yes, I had heard Lord Rex had taken a shine to you. I wasn't aware your relationship had progressed to the point that he'd escort you to an official event."

Lie. One would have to be blind, deaf, and dumb to have missed seeing all the places Rex had escorted Dora. That he was practically living in her abode was also common knowledge. Tabitha, however, wasn't quite ready to accept Dora as one of them.

If Theodora Laurent truly was a money-grabbing, social climber, she'd rush to emphasise her connections with those in the upper echelons of England's class system. Therefore, when Dora spoke, she went the opposite way. She wanted to keep Tabitha off-balance.

"What can I say? The invitation arrived at the last minute. When Rex asked if I was available, I could hardly say no to the poor man. What was I to do? Send him on his own?" Dora shrugged artfully. "I went, expecting a rather staid event. Up until the moment we walked into the Semi-State room, that was exactly what it was. I was so shocked, I could hardly speak. There was your husband, and Lord Clark, who is a dear friend of ours. Poor men, the both of them."

Tabitha blinked back tears. "I still can't believe it. Every time the door opens, I expect Hugh to walk in." Overcome with emotion, she pulled her handkerchief free of her sleeve and dashed the tears washing down her cheeks.

Her pain and suffering were real. Guilt swamped through Dora, making her stomach grow tight. By all rights, she should leave now and let the woman mourn in peace. "I will go," she offered, already rising from her chair.

"No, please don't," Tabitha replied, catching Dora off-guard. "I can't stand to be by myself right now. Everyone else is tiptoeing around me, watching for any signs I'm on the verge of collapse. The only other visitors I've had are the usual gossips, sniffing around for any information they can use to their own benefit."

"And yet, you let me in. Why?" Dora asked, the question slipping out before her mind could second-guess it.

Tabitha lowered the handkerchief to her lap and gave Dora a frank look. "Because you were there. You are my only chance to learn what happened. My brother is too busy protecting my fragile spirits to let slip a single detail. I must understand how this came to pass. Why were you there? What was Lord Clark doing in the room?"

Dora noted Tabitha's words, but she was more interested in the questions she wasn't asking. Tabitha knew why her husband had gone to that room and whom he intended to meet. Clark, Rex, and she were the odd men out.

Dora was not going to leave without getting information. How to do it? Dora's mind raised and discarded tactic after tactic before landing on the one she believed would work best.

There was no better way to coax out secrets than to share

one of your own. Dora would have to be subtle. Tabitha was like a deer on the edge of the woods. Push too hard and she'd run for the safety of the upstairs. Say too little and the deer would remain posed for flight. Lucky for Dora, she was a master of this dance.

"I wish I had answers for all you ask. I, too, have so many questions. When Rex told me Lord Audley arranged for the invite, I had no idea how the night would go."

Tabitha sucked in a short gasp of air. "Lord Audley? He procured your invitation?"

Dora bit her lip, pretending to worry she'd let slip too much. "Yes, but please don't tell anyone. Rex told me we were there to do Lord Audley a favour. He didn't tell me what it was, but when the detective from the Yard interviewed us, Lord Audley mentioned something about Rex keeping an eye on Prince Bertie."

Tabitha pressed her lips together and looked away.

Dora's plan was working.

"Does Lord Rex know Lord Audley well?"

"Lord Audley was his commanding officer during the war. Even now, if Lord Audley asks, Rex obeys."

Tabitha nodded her understanding. Her eyes flicked from left to right and back again. She was at war with herself. How much to say and how much to keep quiet? Her husband was dead... but if Dora was reading the situation correctly, Tabitha might now be at risk. The woman was drowning.

Dora threw her a line. "Do you want me to pass a message along? I'm sure we will see Lord Audley soon, especially since Lord Clark is currently staying with him."

Tabitha lifted her gaze and looked Dora in the eye. Her relief was palpable. "Yes, that would be lovely. Could you ask him to visit? There is a small matter... to do with Hugh, you see.

Thomas will make a hash of it. But Lord Audley — well, his reputation is as sterling as they come."

Tabitha breathed easier now. Dora should leave it there. Let Lord Audley pick up the task of gaining information on exactly how Hugh came to be involved.

But it wasn't in Dora's nature to play second fiddle. Nor did she have time to waste having Lord Audley has a middle man. She needed Tabitha to trust her the way she trusted Lord Audley. It was a risk, but one she was willing to take.

Dora sipped her tea, allowing Tabitha's relief to settle into place. When she spoke, she carefully moderated her tone, making sure not to add any inflection. "That small matter... would it have anything to do with a series of messages?"

Tabitha choked on her tea. "How? But..." Tabitha narrowed her eyes and scrutinised every inch of Dora's face.

Dora took care to make sure she didn't find any reason to tell a lie.

Tabitha leaned closer, her teacup forgotten. All her attention was on the woman sitting across from her. The woman who just might hold the key to her salvation.

"Why yes, yes it does."

Chapter 9
The Anonymous Informant

Rex had long since decided there was nothing worse than being the one left behind to wait. The quiet environs of Dora's comfortable library gave him far too much time to worry. Even having Inga and Harris keep him company did little to dispel his disquiet.

He'd been eyeing the grandfather clock since Dora and Archie had left after luncheon. She'd obviously made it through the front door of the FitzClarence home. He'd watched the half hour and then another pass by with no news.

It was possible she was still chatting... but probable? Rex couldn't imagine a scenario where either woman would want to linger overlong. And yet, Dora was nearing an hour past the time she'd told him to expect her back.

While she was off paying a call to Tabitha FitzClarence, he had decided to spend afternoon tea reading the foreign papers. Dora was adamant that they keep abreast of the latest news from around the world. As she so often said, in their line of work, one never knew where they might end up next.

His choice for the afternoon was to peruse the previous Sunday's edition of the *Berliner Tageblatt*. Ever since he'd admitted his penchant for daydreaming during his German tutorials, Dora had been harping on him to polish his skills. Fortunately, after hours of study, the tongue was coming back to him.

Albeit slowly.

Much like the speed with which the hands moved around that old grandfather clock.

Inga caught Rex glancing up again. "Is there a problem? If you're stuck on something, you have only to ask."

Rex didn't bristle at her offer. He'd long since recognised the wisdom of embracing his shortcomings. He wasn't truly stuck, but perhaps if he asked Inga for help, she'd allow him to draw her into a conversation. That would certainly help pass the time.

Rex handed her the paper, pointing at the article he'd been reading. "The one by Alfred Polgar. I've made it to the fourth paragraph down."

Inga read the lines, mumbling under her breath in a flawless German accent. Then, without missing a beat, she rattled off the translation.

Harris gave Rex a sympathetic smile. "It's no use, man. Our Inga spent half her childhood with her German oma. It's practically her mother tongue."

"Given my mother was part German, there's no practically about it," she quipped in return. "But I'd like to remind you I can do the same trick in French and Italian. If you concentrated less on Cook's scones and more on your language lessons, you could, too."

Rex took care not to look in Harris's direction, lest he be the next one taken to task. Instead, he once again pondered the strange twists in life. He'd certainly never expected to relax in the company of his butler. Nor to dine with the footman. Practising forgery with the upstairs maid was beyond even his wildest childhood imagination. Yet, over the past six months, he'd done all that and more.

All of that had brought him here, to the moment where he had nothing to do but wait. Inga offered him back the paper. He was saved from making further attempts at reading by the arrival of Dora.

Finally!

Although she was perfectly capable of entering a room on silent feet, this time she came in with the force of a storm. Like a cloud heavy with rain, she was bursting with news of her visit.

That didn't mean she was in a hurry to share it. She motioned for them all to fold their papers and put them away while she helped herself to an iced bun and a cup of tea.

"Fair warning," Inga hissed when Dora lifted the bun to her mouth. "That bite will be your last if you prioritise it over telling us your news. Don't bother denying you have something to share. You're so excited, you're practically vibrating."

"Will you permit me a sip of tea to wet my lips before I begin?" Dora batted her lashes.

Inga was unmoved. "One, and be quick. You know I hate it when you make everything into a production."

"Spoilsport!"

Rex caught Harris rolling his eyes at their antics and barely bit back a laugh. He turned it into a cough, but Inga and Dora didn't look in the least convinced. Those two had eyes in the front, back, and sides of their heads.

Dora took the promised single gulp of tea. Then she sat forward, gazing around the room with a sparkle in her eyes. "I know the identity of our anonymous informant."

"Hugh?" Rex asked.

"No," Inga said, lifting a finger to interrupt him. "My money is on Tabitha."

"Right in one, as always." Dora raised her cup in a toast to her best friend.

Inga was so pleased she allowed Dora to eat her iced bun while the rest of them digested her news.

Meanwhile, Rex searched Dora's face for any hint she was less than 100% convinced. He'd long envied her powers of intuition, but she wouldn't be this certain without proof. How would she have found it?

"You searched her house?"

Dora choked on her last bite, so taken aback was she with Rex's accusation. "Of course not! There was hardly any need to resort to trickery when Tabitha was perfectly willing to tell me. It barely required any prodding at all."

"Start at the beginning," Inga instructed, "before you give Rex an apoplexy."

And so Dora did just that.

Rex got comfortable in his chair, the paper at his side long-since forgotten. The most interesting story in the world was the one Dora was recounting in her library.

Dora finished her tale with an assessment of the situation. "You must admit, Tabitha perfectly fits the bill. She is closely connected to Bertie's inner circle twice over, but she doesn't have access to his ear on her own. Hugh was the one to let slip about the other men's stance against the marriage.

"Thomas, Nicholas, and Rupert were determined to convince Bertie to aim higher than Lady Elizabeth. Bertie, however, would hear nothing of it. He'd been starry-eyed for months. They'd counted upon Elizabeth to keep saying no to his proposals. But then she'd shocked them all by saying yes."

"Since they couldn't go to Bertie directly, they decided to manipulate the situation until he had no choice but to call the wedding off." Rex shook his head. "I'm no expert on emotions, but having seen the couple together last night, it is plain as day that Bertie is besotted. And so is she, in return."

"Indeed, which is why Bertie's friends resorted to devious methods. Hugh overheard them discussing and did his best to dissuade them. He told them to leave it be. They promised to stop, but Tabitha didn't buy it. She knew her brother far too well. When he got something in his mind, he was like a dog with a bone. Turns out that deviousness is a talent the twins share. He went to work against Bertie. She began her letter-writing campaign to Lord Audley."

Inga had a question. "Did she say why she chose Lord Audley?"

"Yes. She knew enough of his reputation to be confident he'd have the wherewithal to take action, even in matters at that level. It helped that he isn't exactly known for having a high tolerance for shenanigans."

"Unless you are the one causing them," Inga replied. "So, what went wrong?"

The excitement bled from Dora's face as her mouth turned downwards. "I wish I knew. You can imagine the guilt Tabitha feels right now. I did my best to convince her she was the last person at fault here, but nothing I said got through. Tabitha is as lost as the rest of us. Maybe even more so, given how well she knows all involved."

Rex's stomach clenched, and he regretted his decision to eat a third biscuit. He remembered what it was like to lose someone dear and to feel the pang of regret for things unsaid and undone. Tabitha's situation was much worse. For her sake, as much as anyone else, they had to get to the bottom of this. "Was she able to tell you why Hugh was there instead of her?"

"Tabitha kept her communications with Lord Audley a secret from everyone, including her husband, until the night of the engagement party. She wanted Hugh to accompany her. He was livid, as much because she'd gone behind his back as because she'd dragged in an outsider. He banned her from going."

"A pointless command, I'm guessing," Inga said.

"What makes you say that?" Rex turned to Harris for help, but the other man was equally confounded.

Dora threw her hands in the air. "Any woman strong enough to play games with Lord Audley was hardly going to fall in line because of a cross word from her husband."

"Exactly," Inga agreed. "So, Hugh backed down. Why was he there on his own? And so early?"

"He wanted to go there first, and try to explain the situation, man to man. He promised he'd send for her once he was sure she wasn't going to end up in trouble."

"But instead of a footman with an invitation, she got Thomas coming with the terrible news," Rex guessed rightly.

"She said she took one look at her brother's face and knew it had all gone horribly wrong. But even she couldn't have guessed Hugh's death was a possibility. That's it. You know as much as I do."

Everyone went quiet, each lost in their own thoughts.

Rex couldn't believe that was all of it. There must have been something Dora had left out. "Tabitha must have a guess as to the identity of the killer. Surely she doesn't believe Clark is guilty."

Dora huffed. "Thankfully, she was in full agreement that Clark was framed. She knows it must be one of Hugh's closest friends, but her heart isn't ready to face that."

On that note, Harris rolled up his paper. "I'm disgusted, and it takes a lot for a former police investigator to say that. I've seen crimes of all kinds, but killing your best mate? For what? To stop someone from marrying for love? That's worse than the crime gangs."

Rex had been mulling the same matter. Unlike Harris, he was taking longer than he'd like to come to judgement on the actions of Bertie's friends.

Inga noticed him drumming his fingers on his armrest. "What's on your mind, Rex? These men are your peers."

"The question of murder is black and white. Like Harris, I can't find any justification for it. But the rest..." He twisted in his chair and gazed at Harris, willing him to understand. "Pitting us one against the other and honing our skills at manipulation were part of the unofficial curriculum at school. Then we grew up and went off to war. Every decision we made there was grey and came at a cost. It was a heck of an experience for our formative years.

"Families aren't much better. Since I am the spare, I got a break from it, but my brother must have had hours of listening to lectures about responsibility. The idea of marrying for love never crossed his mind. He wed the eldest daughter of the estate next door because of the land included in her dowry. Believe me, as we dig into this matter, I am sure we'll find that each one of our suspects has a valid reason for standing against Bertie's marriage."

"Rex is right," Dora chimed in. "We cannot be quick to judge anyone lest we alienate a future ally. There isn't a one of us who is a stranger to making impossible decisions under great pressure. We'd do well to remember that."

Rex wished she was exaggerating, even though he knew she was not. The pressure had been gripping their throats since the moment Dora discovered Hugh's cooling body.

Chapter 10
A Gruesome Discovery

ARLIER ON AT THE ENGAGEMENT PARTY
The conductor cleared his throat and announced that the next tune was a waltz. As the dancers filed onto the floor, he turned around and raised his baton to guide the orchestra.

On the other side of the castle ballroom, Dora shuffled closer to the group of older women, counting on their presence to prevent anyone from asking her to dance. Despite her designer gown and upswept coiffure, Dora's presence was strictly business.

It was nearing midnight.

Shortly, Lord Audley would give Prince Bertie the message that someone wanted a word. Until then, Dora was dependent on the help of Harris to make sure everything went to plan.

Like her and Rex, he had an invitation to the royal engagement party. Unlike them, it wasn't to come as a guest. He'd been drafted into the corps of servers circulating around the castle. His assignment was to collect empty glasses where guests abandoned them. Not the most glamorous of work, but it gave him an excuse to wander.

After each of his laps around the Semi-State rooms, he

stopped by the ballroom with an update. Dora made sure she was easy to find.

Lady Edith Bankes-Fernsby, Dowager Duchess of Rockingham, caught Dora's eye and subtly tilted her head. Was all okay?

Dora nodded. Lady Edith smiled and laughed at something another woman had said, seeming to all the world to be engrossed in her conversation. She was a master at lording over her space. No one dared to question the powerful old woman.

That was exactly why Dora had drafted her to their cause. Dora was willing to bet that Edith was better equipped to deal with this particular situation than any trained professional.

Her task was to offer Dora a port of call near the side entrance to the ballroom. She'd taken her responsibilities seriously. Everyone knew she'd taken a shine to her grandson's latest companion. Whereas the other older women of the upper class delighted in turning up their nose at Dora, Edith welcomed her with open arms. Anytime Dora needed to have a quiet word with Harris, Edith provided them with cover.

At this hour, Dora was paying closer attention to the doorway than to the dance floor. She caught a flash of movement. A dark suit and silver tray. That was her cue to step out.

"If you'll excuse me," she murmured. Lady Edith waved her off. The other women were relieved to see the notorious femme fatale go.

Harris was waiting in the next room, empty tray in hand lest anyone question his presence. He strode off without a backward glance, aiming for a quiet corner where they could have a word.

Dora glided behind, pretending to be looking around. He led her through another doorway and into a side passage used by the servants. It was currently empty. After checking no one else was following, she whispered, "Everything as expected?"

"Not exactly. The doors to the Crimson Room are all closed." He leaned closer and dropped his voice even further. "I heard voices. Plural."

Dora was taken aback. She wasn't expecting there to be a second person involved. "What were they saying?"

"Their voices were too muffled for me to make anything out. Best I can say is they were both men."

"Why didn't you open the door?" she hissed, her frustration mounting. The prince was supposed to go to a tête-à-tête. If there were two people involved, that changed the dynamics.

"The guardsman was due to make his circuit. I've had enough trouble as it is not arousing his suspicion. Plus, what if the men inside heard the door opening? I didn't want to flush them out before the rest of you were in place. What good would that do?"

"Fine. You did the right thing. Let's hope it's unrelated. There are plenty of people here looking for quiet places for private conversations. Or more..." She gave Harris a lascivious wink. He had to bite his lip to keep from laughing.

"While you get your amusement under control, I'll make my own loop. We've got a few minutes to spare. With any luck, whoever it is will have moved on." Dora added a last request before heading off. "Meet me on the North Terrace in five minutes. If it is our contact, you can let Lord Audley know exactly where to direct the prince."

Harris opened the door and checked the main hallway before giving Dora the all clear to move. She needed to make haste, but there was the problem of the circulating guards. The Semi-State rooms were enough off the beaten path to require justification for why she was on her own.

Dora searched her memories until she found what she needed. It was the time she'd challenged her brothers to a race during a garden party. Not only had she lost that time, but she'd ripped her dress to shreds in the process. Her mother's fury had known no bounds. She'd dressed Dora down in front of everyone. Even thinking about it now, all these years later, made Dora's cheeks pink with shame.

Fortunately, that was exactly what she needed. When a guard stopped her, she explained she had a desperate need to powder her nose. That trick always worked with men. He pointed her back the way she'd came, but she was having none of it.

"The line is dreadfully long... and I've had several glasses of champers, you see."

"Say no more," the guard begged. "There's another water closet along the next hallway, past the Semi-State rooms. But please, don't wander around. Come straight back when you're done."

Dora promised she'd do exactly that and left before a giggle slipped from her lips. She'd figured out early in her spy career that hinting at lady problems or personal needs was the best way to end a conversation with a man. A useful tip to be sure if one was caught in a desperate situation.

Dora slowed her steps when she entered the corridor leading to the Semi-State rooms. As Harris had said, all along the line the doors were flung open. The only exception was the Crimson Room at the other end.

There were two ways to enter the rooms. The first option was to use the main doors off the corridor. Dora expected Prince Bertie would do that. The second option lay inside the rooms, where she knew there was a series of connecting doors.

Not wanting to be seen, Dora went into the Blue Room. It shared a common wall and a connecting door with the Crimson Room. It was the perfect spot to listen in. If the guard spotted her, she could easily claim she'd got lost on her way to the loo.

Dora pressed her ear to the wooden door.

No sound came through.

She bent over and peered through the keyhole.

There was no one inside.

Dora sighed in relief. Whatever Harris had overheard had been unrelated to their mission. One less problem was never a bad thing...

The thought had barely passed through Dora's mind before she found herself reaching for the doorknob.

It was a risky move. Their informant could show at any moment. Even now, they might be sitting out of sight.

Or... lying in wait.

She twisted the knob with great care and eased the door open a crack. Still no sounds other than the faint strains of violins from the party and the clock inside the room.

She tiptoed in, and that's when she saw him.

Dead.

Dora rushed over to check on the man. He was inordinately still. No breath in his chest. No life in his veins. It was too late to save him.

To save Lord Hugh FitzClarence.

She knew exactly who this was. He was one of Prince Bertie's closest friends.

Dora didn't have the luxury of time to ask questions. Her first instinct was to call everything off. To run for a guard.

But a little voice in the back of her head raised a question. What if this was the message Bertie was meant to get? Was Hugh the informant, or the villain?

They had to let this play out. All of them. But she wouldn't send Rex in unaware.

Dora sprinted across the Crimson Room, dashed through the door, and back into the Blue Room whence she'd come. She closed the doors behind her — the connecting door, the doors to the corridor, even the door to the Emerald Room on the other side. She didn't want anyone else to stumble across the scene.

Harris was waiting for her on the terrace, holding a full tray of empty glasses. Dora slowed her steps as she passed.

"Get Rex and meet me in the Eastern Terrace Garden."

She quickened her pace again, confident he'd do as she said. It was freezing outside, but she didn't feel the cold. Her feet moved as fast as her high heels would allow as she hurried around the corner of the castle wall. She crossed her arms and hugged them tight to keep her white gloves from glowing in the moonlight.

The castle gardens began at the base of the Eastern terrace. This late at night, they were decorated with strangely shaped shadows. For some, it would be the stuff of nightmares. For Dora, they offered safety.

She let the shadows wrap around her like a favourite old cloak. Deeper she went, shivering along the way. She told herself it was from the cold, but she didn't believe her own words.

This straightforward mission had taken a bleak turn. Worse yet, experience told her that this night would get darker still before the day dawned.

Chapter 11
A Brotherly Confession

BACK TO THE INVESTIGATION
Rex could hardly believe his eyes when Dora reached for a second slice of toast. She spread a thick layer of butter across both pieces before drizzling them with honey.

"Darling, as much as I appreciate having your undivided attention, surely we can draw the line at you ogling my breakfast."

"It isn't your breakfast that has me concerned, so much as the amount of training you'll force me to do with you while you work off the energy. Last time you ate that much butter, you made me scale the backside of the house barehanded. Twice."

"That's true... but you know, there are other ways to get our blood pumping," Dora cooed.

"Unfortunately, we pledged to spend our time clearing Clark's name," Rex reminded her. "He sent me a note yesterday evening, begging me to visit him at Lord Audley's. He said the man has him working on papers for the House of Lords. You know how much Clark detests doing actual work."

"And that is exactly why we haven't told him about our undercover activities. It's not that he wouldn't support us, but he'd be forever asking whether we were going out on the town for fun or for a job." Dora took a bite of her toast, somehow managing not to get butter all over her. "On that note, we'd better get our noses to the grindstone. We've got a list of suspects. Where do you want to start?"

"Thomas Liddell?" Rex asked, waiting for Dora's reaction. She nodded her agreement, her mouth too full to answer. "I'd love to know why he sought Bertie out last night."

"And why he chose that particular moment in time," Dora added after a sip of coffee.

"Did Tabitha have any clue?"

"I didn't ask her. Once I got her to speak openly about her role in this whole thing, I didn't want to give her any reason to clam up."

"And pointing out that her twin brother is a prime suspect would have done just that." Rex pushed his plate away, his appetite fading as the complexity of their task set in. "Would you like me to visit Thomas?"

Dora tapped her chin. "Yes, but let's run it past Tabitha first. He can hardly deny a request from her, now can he?" She wiped her hands on her napkin and then stood. "Let's ring her now."

Rex followed behind as Dora made her way to their telephone. She positioned the handset between them so they could both speak and hear.

A footman answered the phone and Rex asked to speak with the duchess. A few minutes later, she came on the line.

"Hello, Tabitha. It's Rex and Theodora. Would it be possible for you to arrange for us to speak with your brother? We have some questions about the engagement party. He was most insistent that he needed to speak with Prince Bertie. We'd like to know why."

"You aren't the only one with unanswered questions,"

Tabitha replied in a sardonic tone. "He's stayed away from me since I got home. I'll ring him now and demand he come round. What do you say? Will half three work for you two?"

Dora confirmed their availability and rang off. "It's not yet noon, Rexy, which means we have plenty of time to get in some exercise."

"I knew you were going to say that," he grumbled. "As long as it doesn't require me to scale walls, I'm in."

"No walls today. We'll practice inside with our rapiers. A few rounds of clashing will provide us with time to sharpen our wits as well."

At least it wasn't reading the foreign papers. Rex and Dora completed their training, enjoyed a light luncheon, and then went out to the car at the appointed time. Thanks to Harris's careful driving, they made it to Tabitha's Mayfair home with a full minute to spare.

This time, the butler allowed Dora to come in without making any comments, although he went out of his way to be extra courteous to Rex. He took Rex's coat and hat, leaving Dora to pass her own off to the footman.

"Her grace and his lordship are in the drawing room," the butler announced in an imperious tone. "Right this way, my lord."

The weighty atmosphere of the well-appointed room made Rex's shoulders slump. Lady Tabitha sat in a chair, upright but with a frown marring her features. Her brother stared into the fireplace, seemingly entranced by the flickering flames. Lady Tabitha invited them to sit. Thomas didn't even turn to acknowledge their arrival.

Rex didn't need to be an expert on social situations to intuit that these two had exchanged harsh words. The room was so tense, even Dora was subdued.

"Allow me to apologise for my brother's poor behaviour. I

told him how I came to be involved in this matter and he's been seething ever since."

"With good reason," Thomas growled, finally turning to face the room. "Hugh is dead! It could have been you, Tabby! We're here because of your actions."

Tabitha blanched at the direct hit, but made no effort to defend herself. Her brother, while angry and afraid for her, would do anything to protect her. Like Rex, he was a man who felt it his duty to take control in times of trouble. Underneath Thomas's anger lay a deep desire to comfort and care for her.

Rex cleared his throat. "That isn't exactly true, Lord Thomas. Hugh is dead because someone is so desperate to stop Bertie's wedding that they were willing to kill. Lady Tabitha was well within her right to take action. The cost Hugh paid was far too high — but it wasn't his fault. Nor your sister's."

Thomas took a moment to process what Rex was saying. Blaming others would get them nowhere and might put his sister at greater risk.

Nodding assent to Rex, Thomas made his way to his sister's side. Kneeling, he took her hand, and with his Adam's apple bobbing, he asked Tabitha to forgive him.

"I will, but only if you take a seat and answer all our questions." Tabitha patted the seat beside hers and waited for him to obey.

Seated together, Rex couldn't help but notice the similarities between the twins. They bore the same dark hair and deep brown eyes. Tabitha's figure was willowy, where Thomas's was lean, but muscular. Even some of their mannerisms were alike.

What would it be like to be so close to a sibling? Rex and his brother had such divergent interests, even as children, that a close friendship was never in the cards. His sister was so much younger that he barely knew her. He'd never envied Dora's relationship with Benedict. Those two bickered more often than they got along. Seeing the twins, for the first time, Rex felt envious of what he'd missed out on.

He shook off his melancholy, knowing now wasn't the time for this line of thought. Later, once all this was resolved, he'd contemplate how he might build a better relationship with his brother and sister.

Dora stepped into the lull in the conversation, posing the first question. "Rex and I were close enough behind you and Prince Bertie to overhear snatches of your conversation. Can you tell us why you sought him out during the party?"

Thomas gritted his teeth and cast a quick glance at his sister. "It was a private matter, and is irrelevant."

Rex caught his movement. "Are you sure it is irrelevant? We heard you mention Hugh's name."

Tabitha shifted in her chair and glared at Thomas. "You were acting strange at the party, following me around and checking up on me. Why? What do you know?"

"I didn't know anything," he declared, raising his hands to fend her off. "But I'm worried about you. You've had these terrible sad expressions on your face when you think no one is looking. You and Hugh have barely come out. Those shadows under your eyes have been there for weeks. Am I supposed to turn a blind eye?" He shook his head. "The only guess I could make was that you were upset because of something Hugh did."

"Something Hugh did? Don't be ridiculous," Tabitha scoffed. "How does any of this relate to you cornering Bertie?"

"I wanted Bertie to speak with Hugh. You know Bertie is the most level-headed of our cohort. Hugh wouldn't lie to him. Frankly, I didn't trust myself not to injure him if he made some kind of confession." Thomas pleaded with his sister, "Please, darling girl, be honest with me. You don't have to protect Hugh any longer. Tell me what he did to make you so despondent."

"I promise — it is nothing Hugh did. He would never hurt me. Quite the opposite."

"Then why won't you tell me what is wrong? You can hardly claim privacy when you've just forced my hand."

"We can step out," Rex said, half-rising from his chair. Dora would likely thrash him later for offering, but he was too much of a gentleman to openly listen in to a private family matter.

"No. Stay. All of you. What's done is done." Tabitha took a deep breath to steady her nerves. She stared straight ahead, not daring to meet anyone's gaze. "Hugh and I had news... good news. We were waiting to share until we were sure. But... it wasn't meant to be. We took it hard. Both of us, but me more so. It had to be my fault. Something wrong with me. Hugh told me no, over and over again. He was my rock, not my source of pain."

Thomas slid out of his seat and fell to his knees in front of Tabitha's chair. "Oh, my dearest, I had no idea. I'm so sorry, so awfully sorry. You should have told me. No, I should have asked. How did you bear that on your own?"

Tabitha stroked her brother's cheek. "I wasn't alone. Not then, anyway. It wasn't something you could fix. Our burden was so great, we didn't want to put it on anyone else's shoulders. Now, it is mine alone to bear."

Thomas flinched when Tabitha choked back a sob. He clasped her hands and made his promise. "I will stay with you. You know that. You will never be alone, not so long as I draw breath."

Tabitha gave him a watery smile. She pulled her hands free and wiped her cheeks.

Rex felt like a voyeur sitting there with a front-row seat at such an intimate moment. He and Dora held still, not wanting to intrude.

Tabitha wasn't finished. She calmed herself and then addressed her brother. "Thomas, we are the same age, but in many ways, you are still a child. Dear as you are, you can never take the place of my beloved husband. You, too, must one day marry and start a family of your own. So please, do not make promises you cannot keep."

Tabitha lifted her gaze and glanced at Rex and Dora. "This is why Hugh refused to take part in his friend's plans to ruin Bertie's relationship. As the only married man in the bunch, he best understood Bertie's motives for asking for Elizabeth's hand."

Thomas had no idea what she meant, but Rex did.

Tabitha rolled her eyes at her brother's foolhardiness. "I'm talking about love."

"Love?" Thomas reared back at his sister's reply. "There's no place for sentimental emotions in our set. We have a duty to uphold our family line, to marry well and gain stature."

"Poppycock!" Tabitha's cheeks burned. She pushed him away and stood, too annoyed to sit still. "Our parents muttered those lines repeatedly until I believed them. I married Hugh because he fitted the bill. We thanked the Lord every day for the joy we eventually found."

"That sort of happiness it isn't in the cards for me, as you well know." Thomas rocked back on his heels and threw his hands in the air.

Although he never said the words, Rex knew what he was saying. He'd heard the rumours about Lord Thomas's predilections. Apparently, they were true. Among their generation of gentleman, everyone was willing to turn a blind eye. But that wouldn't remove Thomas's obligations to his family.

Thomas's thoughts followed the same line. "I must do my duty. I will inherit Father's title. I must ensure it passes along. If I am to find joy, I must do so outside of marriage. If you ask me, Bertie should do the same."

"If I could make the world safe for you, I would, dearest brother of mine. But alas, that task is far too great for someone as insignificant as I am. I don't know what saddens me more — that you will never be able to publicly admit which way you lean, or that you would sentence Bertie to the same."

Thomas clutched his chest as her barb hit home.

"What Bertie and Elizabeth have found is something to be protected and treasured. Hugh and I understood. Bertie's life will never be easy — royal life rarely is, despite how it might seem from the outside. Elizabeth will stand at his side. I pray that someday, you will have someone in your life who does loves you that way."

Tabitha's wisdom was undeniable. Yet Rex felt a smidgen of sympathy for Thomas. Less than a year earlier, Rex had been standing in those same shoes. Unaware of what it meant to be in love and to be loved. Not because of family connections, but for who he was when no one else was around.

It had taken him and Dora time to work up the courage to give a relationship a try. Once they'd given in to the longings of their hearts, there was no chance of them turning back. Suddenly, the thought of spending the rest of his life with one woman no longer seemed scary.

Rex couldn't have stopped himself from glancing at Dora if he'd tried. A rush of pleasure coursed through him when he caught Dora doing the same.

Tabitha gave a polite cough to get their attention. "You two know what I mean. That's why I trust you will help me."

"Help you with what?" Thomas asked, still lost.

"Protecting Bertie and Elizabeth. Finding out who killed Hugh. Ensuring peace for an entire nation."

For Rex and Dora, that was all in a day's work.

Chapter 12
The Unpaid Debt

After a night of sleep, the household prepared to take on their next task — raising Clark's spirits. The poor chap was so morose, Lord Audley himself had phoned and invited them over for lunch. It was a rare occasion where they'd been encouraged to use the front entrance.

Never one to miss out on a special event, even if it was one with a limited audience, Dora took great care when selecting her clothing for the day. She had to ask the housemaid for help getting dressed. She didn't want Inga or Rex to know what she'd chosen until she was ready to make her grand entrance.

At the strike of the hour, Dora glided down the stairs to the foyer, held out her arms, and spun around so Rex could get the full effect. "How do I look?"

"Like a pot of gold at the end of the rainbow," Rex answered. "But aren't you a tad overdressed for the occasion?"

Dora glanced down at the gold silk dress with fringed beads decorating the neckline and the hem. "Can anything ever be too much when it comes to Clark? Between being a suspect in a murder and living in forced captivity with Lord Audley, the poor man must be desperate for some good news."

Inga stepped out of the drawing room with her coat and hat in hand. "So we're taking him to Oz? If you are playing the role of the good witch, I hope you don't expect me or Rex to be the scarecrow."

"Of course not. You are much better suited to be the Tin Man."

Harris arrived then, carrying Dora and Rex's outer garments. He stopped beside Inga and gave her a smacking kiss on the cheek. "My darling girl has the biggest heart of us all. Otherwise, there's no way she'd put up with us."

"Comments like that will earn you a reward for good behaviour."

"That's what I'm counting upon." Harris leered at Inga. She swatted his arm, and they all laughed.

"And on that note, we should be on our way. Lead on, Miss Laurent," Inga said, sounding more like an army sergeant than a companion.

Her fierce tone reminded Dora of the head nurse when they'd been stationed at the front. Sister Gertrude was more fearsome than the shouting doctors or the distant sounds of the heavy artillery. Many a night, she and Inga had entertained themselves by doing impersonations. It seemed Inga had finally mastered Sister Gertrude.

They completed the drive in good time, continuing to tease one another good-naturedly. It wasn't that they were ignorant of the pressure of time, nor the risk of further problems looming on the horizon. They knew from experience that these moments of levity were required to protect their sanity.

They burst into Lord Audley's, barely pausing long enough to allow his butler to get out of the way. Their evident good humour cracked the icy silence. Dora's tinkling laugh spread through the house like the first tendrils of spring.

Clark and Lord Audley were waiting in the study. Clark

brightened at the sight of his friends. Dora took satisfaction from his smile. "Lord Audley, I don't suppose we could convince you to look the other way? Instead of lunch here, we could all dash out for one of our adventures."

Lord Audley glowered at her, playing his role of jailer to the hilt. "And leave my reputation in tatters? I think not."

The butler's arrival prevented any further discussions. He stuck out his chest and made his pronouncement. "Luncheon is served in the dining room, Your Grace."

Lord Audley's dining room was furnished in the Edwardian style, from the heavily carved chair legs to the marble inlays on the table and robin's egg blue walls. While the footman poured the wine and set plates in front of them all, Dora eyed the colourful swirls on the porcelain vase acting as a centrepiece. Like the candlesticks on either side, the items were far too feminine to have been selected by Lord Audley. Yet, they were also far too new to have been part of his inherited estate.

These were vestiges of Lord Audley's brief marriage. Dora knew the story. His wife had died in a riding accident before they'd had children. Everyone expected Lord Audley to remarry, but he'd been content to let his brothers' sons carry on the family name. He threw himself into his work.

Would Dora be sitting at that table if his Duchess had survived? Perhaps, but she doubted that she'd be there as Theodora Laurent.

Like it or not, death often caused ripples that continued long past the official period of mourning. Would Lord Hugh's death be the same? Dora thought Tabitha might emerge a different woman, her spirit tempered by the flames of tragedy. She certainly showed all the signs of having the right temperament to keep going.

But now wasn't the time to worry about Tabitha. Dora turned her attention back to Lord Clark. She needed to take his mind off his current troubles. The best way to do so was to remind him of all the things he'd got away with. She searched her memory for something appropriate — heavy on the mischief, light on the harm. A story came to mind.

"Clark, have you confessed to Lord Audley about the time you replaced all the vases in the dining hall at the House of Lords with displays of pineapples?"

Clark launched into the tale, just as she'd intended. There was nothing that man liked better than being the centre of attention. Well, so long as he wasn't at the centre because he was accused of murder.

Rex jumped in from time to time to correct Clark when his exaggerations became too much, or he veered too close to something that might land him in hot water. Meanwhile, they enjoyed a lavish four-course meal prepared by Audley's excellent chef. After a dessert of mulled winter fruits with cinnamon ice cream, Audley led them to the billiards room for an afternoon of games. He was on the verge of taking his leave when the butler knocked on the door.

"A DCI Miller is here, Your Grace. He would like a word with Lord Clark."

"Show him in. I'm sure we're all interested to see what the man has to say."

Dora and Rex again flanked Clark, while Inga took the next nearest seat. DCI Miller would find his prey well protected should he think to press the issue of Clark being a suspect.

"Perhaps he's here to tell me I'm free to return home," Clark said in a hopeful tone.

Dora, however, was less convinced. If that was all he had to say, he could send a message or telephone.

No, the man was there for a different purpose.

DCI Miller's heavy tread preceded him into the room. His stern expression matched his dark grey coat and the black trilby tucked under his arm. His presence was enough to leech the joy from the room. Even Dora's golden dress couldn't compete.

Lord Audley did not invite the man to sit down, nor did the butler offer to take his coat and hat. He wasn't there for a friendly visit, and they didn't intend to let him linger any longer than necessary.

DCI Miller was unperturbed. He pulled his notepad from his pocket after Lord Audley finished introducing Inga.

Dora took the measure of the man. His questions would reveal as much about his investigative skills as whatever he intended to gain from asking Clark more questions.

DCI Miller inclined his head at Lord Audley, showing only the slightest hint of obeisance to the highly placed duke. "Apologies for intruding on your get together, Your Grace. I won't take too much of your time."

"Carry on," Audley instructed.

"I have a few questions about how well Lord Clark knew Lord Hugh." DCI Miller pinned Clark with his stern gaze. "Would you say that you were friends?"

Clark's first attempt at answering came out as a whisper. He cleared his throat and tried again. "Acquaintances would be more accurate. He was a friend of Prince Bertie, as you well know. I've been known to go out carousing with Prince Edward from time to time. Every now and again, our paths crossed. Like last night at the party," Clark was quick to add. "We were both there at the invitation of the royal family."

"What of the night of January fifth?"

Dora felt Clark tremble. She leaned closer to shore his spirits.

Clark scrunched his brow and thought hard. He was overplaying his hand, as far as Dora was concerned. He knew exactly which day DCI Miller meant, even if he pretended otherwise.

"I don't remember doing anything of significance that evening. I can check my diary if you'd like."

"There's no need. Perhaps this will jog your memory. You visited the Strachey home. I believe you participated in a game of cards."

Clark paled. "That's possible. I go there often, as Rex can confirm. If I'm remembering the night correctly, it was a normal evening out."

"Was it normal for you to lose £200?"

Rex winced. Audley, Dora, and Inga didn't move. Beads of sweat dotted Clark's forehead. DCI Miller, still in his winter coat, was cool as ice.

"That was a higher loss than normal, but I'd have won it back. Hugh had the luck of the gods that night, but they rarely bestow their favour for longer than that. I'm sure that within a fortnight, the money would have found its way back to my pocket."

"Only if you had made good on the debt. But you did not. Is that why you killed him? Because you couldn't pay? Did he threaten your reputation?"

Clark threw his hands up to stop the torrent of tough questions. "I forgot. I was inebriated that night. It wasn't until I saw Hugh again at the engagement party that I remembered. You were there, Rex. Remember? I told you as soon as I saw Hugh enter the ballroom."

Rex rushed to Clark's defence. "I know £200 seems like a lot of money to throw around. It must be what, a year's pay on your salary? But Clark was good for it. He's rung up much higher tallies in the past."

"Lord Clark's gambling habits are not relevant to this case," Audley said, intervening before Rex could let anything else slip. "His family does not suffer from a shortage of funds. Do you have any other questions, DCI Miller?"

"No, not for now."

"Excellent. In that case, I have one of my own to pose. Are you exploring other lines of investigation as part of this inquiry?"

Dora paid close attention, but DCI Miller was too much a professional to give anything away.

He put his notebook away and pulled his cap from under his arm. "It's early days, and there are many leads. I don't know yet which one will lead to a conviction. There is nothing to say that this one is a dead end. And on that note, Lord Clark, I expect you to stay put. I'll see myself out."

Clark began shaking before they heard the echo of the front door closing. Dora, Rex, and Inga reassured him that they all knew he was innocent. They promised it would all work out okay in the end.

Rex forced a measure of whiskey at his friend, telling him it would calm his nerves. Clark's hand continued to shake as he took the crystal glass. "I must say this again. I am eternally grateful for your friendship. Especially now, during this difficult time."

Dora had great sympathy for Clark. But she also felt for DCI Miller. Although they were on opposite sides of the field, both men were pawns in a larger game.

Unfortunately, her hands were tied. She couldn't tell either of them the real reason she knew Clark was innocent.

When someone had shoved a knife into Hugh's heart, Clark had been speaking with Rex in the ballroom.

Chapter 13
The Mountain Visits

Rex supposed he could describe his occupation as playing cat and mouse, but rarely did he mean it as literally as today. It wasn't his fault... not entirely, anyway. But he didn't favour his chances if forced to explain to Dora why there was a mouse in the breakfast room.

He'd started off with the best of intentions. The heavy clouds that had obscured the morning sun had finally decided to shed their weight. When the first raindrops hit the window, Rex leapt to his feet and rushed to the terrace door. Mews was outside, and would be most displeased to be left to the elements.

The damp cat had rushed past him with a grateful meow and plopped onto the warm carpet. When Rex turned to check on him, he caught sight of their unintended guest — a small, grey mouse. Mews spat it onto the carpet and then sat back, waiting to be praised. The half-stunned mouse got to its feet and scurried under the nearby ebony hutch.

Rex had acted fast. He slammed shut the doors to the corridor and banned the staff from coming inside. He'd solve this because he simply had to do so. Dora wasn't Mews's biggest fan on the best of days.

"Get to your feet, old pal, and help me out," Rex cajoled Mews. It was no use. The cat was more interested in drying its fur than in chasing its prey. After all, it wasn't as though the mouse was leaving anytime soon. There was surely a lesson in all this, but Rex wasn't in the right frame of mind to examine it.

He spent ten fruitless minutes moving one piece of furniture, only to have the mouse sprint for cover under another. The situation required reinforcements. He cornered the mouse on the far side of the room and then opened the door and bellowed for Archie. He didn't shift his focus from the mouse's current hiding spot until Archie was inside the room.

The men pulled together a strategy. Working in concert, they'd herd the mouse toward the open terrace door and hope it ran for freedom.

It was a fool-proof plan with one fatal flaw. Mews.

Rex and Archie had the mouse crisscrossing its way toward the exit. It was nearly to the door when Mews spotted the dark tuft of fur skittering across the carpet.

Mews pounced.

The mouse reared back and changed direction, doing a 180 degree spin toward the opposite side of the room.

Rex's luck ran out.

At the same moment, blithely unaware of the chaos inside, Dora opened the breakfast-room door.

"Oi!" Archie shouted.

"Watch out!" Rex chimed in.

Without a second thought, Dora bent over and swiped up the mouse seconds before it would have run across her slippered foot. She cooed at the little darling as she waltzed past the open-mouthed men and urged it to run for the safety of the rear garden.

Of course, the rain had stopped almost as quickly as it had begun. Other than a single puddle on the stone pavers, there was no evidence to back up Rex's story of how a mouse ended up inside.

Dora, however, was far too amused to be mad. The sight of the burly men, dishevelled and sweaty after their fruitless battles, sent her into gales of laughter. By the end of it, Rex could almost see the funny side of the situation.

Almost, but not quite. At least he wasn't in trouble. That was what mattered in the end.

After dusting himself off, Rex glanced at the clock and then leaped for the door. "Good heavens, is that the time? We're due at my grandmother's in less than 15 minutes."

"Settle down. There's no need for us to go to the mountain today. The mountain has decided to come to us."

Rex wondered if he'd bumped his head earlier and forgotten about it. "I'm sorry. Did you just say that my grandmother is coming here? Before noon? She'll end up on the front page of the gossip rags."

"You underestimate your grandmother. She is just as enamoured of undercover work as I am. As far as the world is convinced, the dowager duchess is at home, tucked away in her bed at this ungodly hour. Edith, however, will use the servants' entrance to see her friends Dora and Inga."

Rex was struck once again by Dora's ability to sway even the tightest-laced individual to her way of living. Although, perhaps his grandmother was not the best example. She revelled in keeping society on their toes. It hadn't taken much of a push to get her to break free of what little constraints held her in check.

How would Dora do with the rest of his family? He couldn't imagine his father and brother having any interest in her, despite her good looks and colourful background. Those two had always preferred to spend their days riding horseback or partaking of other manly pursuits. His mother, a flighty thing, would be completely overwhelmed by her effervescent personality.

What about his sister, Caledonia? Rex could barely picture her in his mind. Nearly a decade younger, he'd been off at school by the time she could walk and talk. The rare times he went home for summer, Nanny sent him to cavort in the sunshine while his sister stayed in with her dolls. The last few visits, she'd been off at school. She must be near grown by now, yet he still pictured her as a young girl. He was ashamed to admit, even if only to himself, how little he knew about his younger sibling.

Dora's voice cut into his deep thoughts and pulled him back to the present. She asked Archie to pour Rex another cup of coffee. "Maybe the caffeine will help you stay focused."

Rex apologised. "I got lost in my thoughts about the rest of my family. At some point, I should introduce you to them. I'll talk to Grandmama about it. She'll know how to best arrange things."

Dora was caught off guard. "Your family? Meeting Theodora Laurent? Do you think that is smart? How much would you even tell them?"

"I'll tell them how amazing you are and how much brighter my life is with you in it. I want them to know I intend to spend the rest of my days with you for as long as you're willing to have me."

Dora was genuinely touched. She embraced him and whispered in his ear, "Your words outshine all the diamonds in the world, even if you speak of impossibilities. It's enough for me that your grandmother supports us. Let's leave the rest of your family for the future."

Rex let her pull away, but he wasn't as ready to abandon the idea as she was. Perhaps it was all the talk of marriage and commitment, but he couldn't set aside his desire to let the world know how he felt about her. How they felt about each other.

This thought lingered in his mind while they walked through the house to the conservatory, where they were to await his grandmother.

Shortly after, she arrived in a burst of cold air, shivering while unbuttoning her cheap wool coat. At Rex's raised eyebrow, she explained, "I borrowed this from a housemaid who is of a similar size. After experiencing just how little protection it is against the frigid January wind, I'm of mind to procure new coats for all the below-stairs staff."

"You'd best make it part of their official uniform so they'll be more likely to accept the gift," Dora suggested. Edith thought that was a capital idea.

Harris brought in a steaming pot of tea to warm the dowager, and they all sat. Dora and Rex chose a wicker divan while Edith sat on a comfortable wooden chair positioned in a patch of sunshine next to the radiator.

They brought Edith up to speed on the latest information. Like them, she knew Clark was innocent, so they didn't waste any time telling her of DCI Miller's findings. Instead, they updated her on Tabitha and Thomas.

"Those two always were two peas in a pod. At one point, I worried Tabatha would choose not to marry. Fortunately, Thomas came across a handy solution. By arranging a marriage between her and Hugh, he ensured she'd forever remain close but not alone." Her voice trailed off. "His intentions were good, even if life intervened."

Silence fell over the group. Rex noticed his grandmother blinking back tears. She was the only one of them to have experienced the loss of a spouse. Rex moved to go comfort her, but she waved him off.

"Back to business, if you please. Who is left on your suspect list?"

Knowing his grandmother did not want to show any weakness, Rex agreed to her request to move the conversation along. "Nicholas and Rupert hold joint position at the top."

"And if it is neither of them?"

"Then we'll look more closely into Hugh's other associates."

"And Prince Bertie's," Dora added. "I have many questions. No one else knew Hugh was going to that room. They certainly couldn't have known why Hugh went there. So what made our killer act? Did one of his friends stab Hugh to prevent him from telling Bertie about their treachery? Or did a stranger stab Hugh for some other unknown reason? We can see the full picture, but could anyone else?"

"One step at a time," Edith replied. "My web stretches from one end of this town to the other. Sooner or later, we'll find a critical connection."

Rex agreed. "Let's begin with you telling us what you know of Nicholas and Rupert."

"I will start with Rupert because I know the least about him. His father is Sir Arthur Simpson. Made his fortune in manufacturing and earned the honorary after the Great War."

"In that case, how did he end up running in the same sphere as the royal family?" Dora asked.

"His mother is the former Lady Helen Clarence, youngest daughter of Lord Clarence. Lady Helen has been friends with Lady Elizabeth's mother since girlhood. Both families are from up north. Lady Elizabeth is likely the reason why Prince Bertie and Rupert became such good friends while at school. They had her in common."

"What of Rupert's reputation?" Rex asked.

"Clean as a whistle, although that should come as no

surprise. None of Bertie's friends run with the fast set, as you well know."

"And yet, one of them is almost certainly up to no good."

"Fair point," Edith conceded. "Unfortunately, I can't tell you what lies in any of their hearts. I'll consult my resources and report back."

Rex thanked her for the help. "You said you knew less of Rupert. That implies you have something more to tell us about Nicholas."

"Not so much about him as his family. His father is a duke and his mother a princess — in Belgium. She relinquished the title when she married. When you speak with Nicholas, I suggest you ask about his cousin Princess Marie."

"Another familial relationship," Rex grumbled. "Can you give us a little more in case he proves reticent?"

"Of course, I can. I know for a fact that Princess Marie of Belgium made Queen Mary's shortlist of approved royal brides."

"Really! So you think he may have his nose out of joint because she was passed over in favour of a lower-titled lady?"

"All I can offer is a place to start. It is up to the two of you to see where the questions take you." Having fulfilled her duties, Edith rose from her chair.

"Are you leaving us so soon, Grandmama?"

"Hardly!" Edith replied, walking not to the exterior door but toward the main part of the house. "I'm staying at least through lunch. Inga has promised to teach me how to play billiards."

Rex covered his face and groaned, causing Dora to giggle. He was outnumbered and out-manoeuvred by the women in his life.

Still, he made an attempt at talking sense into his grandmother. "At the rate you are going, you're going to end up running with the fast set."

Edith stood tall, unbent by her grandson's chastising. "If I were a few decades younger, I'd give you all a run for your money."

"Don't kid yourself," Dora said, causing Edith to raise her eyebrows. "Given how active your social life is now, it's us who would struggle to keep up. Now, don't let Inga convince you to play for money."

An evil grin crossed Edith's lined face. "Don't worry, dear. I won't do anything you wouldn't do."

Rex barely held back a grin when Dora's mouth dropped open as his grandmother gave her a taste of her own medicine. In truth, he didn't know whether to laugh or despair over his grandmother's Dora-inspired antics.

Chapter 14
More Royal Entanglements

After a brief discussion, Dora and Rex agreed that, once again, Tabitha was their best asset. Dora offered to give her a ring to discuss how to proceed. Together, they walked to the telephone.

In Dora's house, the rule was whoever was nearest answered any calls. One never knew when it might be an emergency. This wasn't the case at the home of Duke and Duchess FitzClarence.

Before Dora could speak with Tabitha, she had to make it past the gatekeeper, also known as the FitzClarence's formidable butler. Dora assumed her burgeoning friendship with Her Grace would be enough to convince him to put Tabitha on the line. That's why she gave her name at the start of the call.

"Her grace is not available to take any calls," he announced in an impervious tone.

Tabitha couldn't be out. She was in mourning. Dora nibbled her lower lip. "Is she unwell?"

"Her grace is the picture of health. She is, I repeat, *unavailable.*"

The *to you* was heavily implied.

Dora had options available. She could put Rex on the line, and have him force the butler's hand. But that would only end up making them all look small and petty. She saw no benefit to a Pyrrhic victory in her war with the stuffy old man.

"I see. Please let her know I rang," she asked, and replaced the receiver without giving him a chance to reply.

"What now?" Rex asked. "Shall I give it a go? Surely he won't decline my call."

Dora tapped her chin. "I've got a better idea." With no explanation, she hurried to the game room and asked Edith if she could spare a moment.

This time around, the conversation with the butler went in a more productive direction.

"Good morning, this is the Dowager Duchess of Rockingham phoning. With whom do I speak?"

"Good morning, Your Grace. I'm the FitzClarence butler. How may I be of assistance?"

"I'd like to speak with Lady FitzClarence," Edith explained, adding, "if it isn't too much trouble."

This time around, the butler was falling all over himself in his eagerness to please. "Of course, Your Grace. Right away. Shall I tell her why you're ringing?"

"It is regarding my grandson, Lord Rex. He and Miss Laurent are going out of their way to help Her Grace, and yet Lady FitzClarence can't see fit to take their calls. I'd like to know why."

The man's gulp was audible. "I beg your pardon, Your Grace. I believe there has been some kind of mistake. The duchess was unavailable at the moment they rang. She is, as I've said, available now."

"I see. I expect her to be available at all times, within reason, of course," Edith's stern tone brooked no argument. "I'll ring off to let them know they can reach the duchess now."

Dora bit her knuckles to keep from laughing aloud. Edith had outdone herself, just as she'd expected. When she rang again a few minutes later, she had no trouble getting through. Tabitha was pleased enough by her call, blithely unaware of what had transpired.

"We'd like to speak with Rupert and Lord Nicholas. Do you have any advice on how to best approach them?"

"Rupert is a man's man," Tabitha explained. "He sent a condolence note, of course, but other than that, I've not seen or heard from him."

"Very well. Rex can track him down. How about Lord Nicholas?"

"It just so happens that he is coming round today. There are a few books Hugh would want him to have."

"Would you mind terribly if we pulled the same trick again with me and Rex turning up after his arrival?"

"Nick will speak more freely if you come alone and I vouch for you. Why don't you come again at 3:30? When he arrives, I'll tell him what a great comfort you've been."

"Let's hope he buys that."

"Theodora, I won't need to lie. Knowing you and Rex have picked up the banner is of great relief to me."

"Thank you for saying that, Tabitha. We won't let you down, no matter what it takes."

Dora rang off. Rex had overheard the entire conversation.

"What shall we do about Rupert?" Rex asked.

"Benedict wants to help. Ask him to arrange an encounter." Dora added, "Schedule it for tomorrow. With any luck, I'll have some tidbits from Nicholas that you can use to direct your inquiry."

Without delay, the pair split to go about the rest of their normal activities. The spies seemed to wander between parties, but they had plenty to do in secret. After all, it did little good to send them in high-level conversations if they didn't have the background information to make sense of what they learned.

They enjoyed a late luncheon with Edith and Inga before Dora left to visit Tabitha.

Dora dressed with even greater care than normal, opting for a bias-cut, forest green afternoon dress by Vionnet. Black Mary Janes and a wool felt cloche completed the look.

Harris was waiting inside the Rolls-Royce. He stayed silent during the drive, knowing she'd want time to focus on her tasks. Although Dora gazed out the window, she paid no notice to the cars, buses, and people they passed.

Instead, she imagined the role she needed to play in order to convince Nicholas to take her into his confidence. None of her normal tricks for getting past a man's defences were appropriate given the circumstances. Theodora had to be subtle, trustworthy, and earnest – none of which were things for which she was known. Theodora was going to have to be... Dorothy.

Dora had not thought about her real identity in quite some time. She'd been playing the role of the French socialite for so long that it now felt completely natural.

But Tabitha FitzClarence would never befriend someone of Theodora's ilk. Dorothy Cavendish, daughter of the Duke of Dorset, was a far more appropriate friend. The irony of the situation was not lost on Dora. No matter how far she tried to run from what society deemed appropriate, she found herself drawn back to playing the game.

The worst of it was that Tabitha was someone Dora actually liked, based on what she'd seen so far. Tabitha stood up for her principles, had a backbone made of iron, and a determination to make the best of whatever life threw her way.

Still, Dora could hardly drop the light French accent she'd adopted as part of her persona. Nor could she confess about her double life as an undercover spy.

However, there was nothing saying she couldn't allow some of her childhood lessons on how to keep from scaring a man off to shine through. Her nanny had been most insistent that Dora master the ability to temper her worst instincts. Thanks to her, she could bite her tongue while still keeping a smile on her face.

That skill, combined with her genuine admiration for Tabitha, would have to be enough to convince Nicholas to reveal... well, whatever she could pry out of him.

Harris spun the steering wheel, turning the sleek car onto Tabitha's street. Dora stilled her racing mind by forcing herself to count breaths. When she stepped out of the car in front of Tabitha's front gate, she had fully embodied the persona she'd chosen.

Dora was a few minutes early, but she saw no point in waiting in the car. The butler opened the door and took her coat without a word or a nod of respect, and gave it to a footman. He led her past the doorway to the drawing room, instead guiding her deeper into the grand home. A carpet runner muted their footsteps as they walked past busts on pedestals and framed portraits. Dora was so caught up in who the people in the portraits might be that it took her a moment to realise she was staring at Tabitha's face.

It wasn't a painting. Tabitha had opened a door just as Dora walked past. Framed by the doorway, she was as pale as the powdered faces of the FitzClarence's Elizabethan ancestors. Tabitha flushed in embarrassment, but she still looked frail.

Dora knew she was supposed to remain quiet, but Tabitha wouldn't withstand a strong breeze in her current state. Concerned, Dora asked if they should reschedule.

"No, I'm fine. My discomfort has passed. I'll be better once I've had some tea." With that, Tabitha asked the butler to see to tea. She then led Dora to the private sitting room.

This room was smaller than the drawing room, and

furnished more comfortably, but no less expensively. The choice of location was no accident. It was a silent way for Tabitha to communicate that Dora had made it past the first stage of friendship.

Dora kept a close eye on Tabitha, but as promised, she perked up as her skin took on a rosier tone while sipping a cup of tea and munching on a ginger biscuit. The two women didn't have long to strategise before they heard the peal of the doorbell. The butler escorted Nicholas back to them shortly after.

Nicholas was caught off guard, to say the least. He veered close to Tabitha, almost acting as her protector, until she told him to have a seat.

He settled down once Tabitha explained how much Dora's visits had helped her. "We are each going through hard days," Tabitha explained. "Between my loss and Theodora being worried about her dear friend Lord Clark, we found common ground."

Nicholas grimaced. He, too, felt for Clark. "I can't imagine that he's guilty, but equally, I can't imagine anyone wanting to hurt Hugh. I'm just glad that Scotland Yard's finest are looking into the case."

Dora used his remark to segue into the direction she wanted to go. "I happened to be visiting with Clark yesterday when the detective paid him a call. DCI Miller had some questions about you, Nicholas," she added, fibbing a little.

Nicholas was taken aback. "About me? Why?"

"If Clark isn't the killer, he believes it must be someone well-known to Hugh. There were no signs of a struggle."

Nicholas still professed to be at a loss. "I could never hurt Hugh or any of my friends."

Tabitha chided him. "What about Bertie and his engagement? I know you disagreed with it. You and the others had every intention of doing whatever it took to prevent him from marrying Lady Elizabeth. No matter the cost to Bertie."

Nicholas shook his head. "That's different. It wasn't a personal matter, but one of state."

"So, it had nothing to do with your cousin being passed over for the role of royal bride?" Dora asked.

Nicholas flinched. Dora was sure they'd struck home.

"Was that why you did this? As some sort of retaliation against the palace? Be honest with us, Nicholas," Tabitha instructed. "If the detective is as good as everyone claims, he will almost certainly find out. I can help you if you tell me everything. You can trust Theodora as well."

"No, no, that isn't why I tried to talk Bertie out of his marriage plans. I intervened because he refused to listen to anyone else. The only reason I discovered Marie was on the potential bride list was because Bertie told me. His father sent it to him with instructions to select one. As though he were ordering a dish from a menu. Bertie was so livid he could barely get a word out."

Bertie's stutter had the bad habit of rearing its head at the worst moments. In his shoes, she'd have been apoplectic.

"What did you tell him?" Tabitha asked.

Nicholas's eyebrows shot up. "What do you think? I said he should follow orders! He is as much a royal subject as the rest of us. If the king said to pick a wife, he'd be mad to ignore the edict."

"But he did just that. Why do you think he chose to ignore his father this time?"

"I haven't the faintest bloody clue!" Nicholas erupted before fighting to regain control. He apologised for the harsh language. "I'm not blind. I've seen how he and Elizabeth look at one another. But I also know what kind of man the king is. He does not tolerate disobedience."

"But Bertie is the second son, not the heir," Tabitha reminded him.

"So, too, is our reigning king. His older brother died unexpectedly, and he found himself in line for the throne. He even married his brother's intended. No, he'd be the last person on this earth to view love as a rationale for any decision. Given my family's connections to Europe's royal courts, I understood better than anyone. It didn't matter to me one whit whether he chose Marie or someone else, as long as he picked from the list."

Dora couldn't find a lie or half-truth hidden in Nicholas's answers. Still, she wasn't going to let go of the one lead they had.

"What of Marie? Did you tell her she made the cut?"

"There was no point. Bertie dithered for so long, proposing to Elizabeth time and time again, that Marie agreed to alternate arrangements. She's to marry into the Spanish royal family. They will announce the engagement in due time."

It was a good explanation, especially because it would be difficult to prove. It wasn't as though Dora could phone the royal house of another country and ask pointed questions. That didn't mean all was lost. Dora was certain Edith could verify the matter through one connection or another.

For now, however, there was nothing to be gained from further prying. Having reached a dead end, Dora turned the conversation onto other matters... namely Rupert. Thomas and Nicholas had ready explanations for why they had interceded in the wedding matter. Would Rupert be as fast on his feet? Dora trusted Rex to find out.

Chapter 15
A Night on the Town

After only five minutes in the car, Rex was already regretting his decision to bring Benedict along. Why'd he let Dora convince him this was a good idea? Yes, he could always use a second set of eyes, but life was so much better when those eyes were in her head.

Instead, he was stuck with Dora's recalcitrant brother. From the moment Benedict had heard their destination, he'd launched into a litany of complaints.

"The Stracheys? Are you certain?" Benedict cupped his ear, feigning hearing loss. "You misheard. I can't imagine anyone from Bertie's set crossing the threshold into that den of iniquity."

Rex's valet might not know everything, but when it came to ferreting out a man's evening plans, there was no one better. "Brantley assured me the information was valid. He got it directly from Rupert's own valet. He's expected at the Strachey home. Our only challenge is figuring out which one."

The Strachey brothers were building an empire around Gordon Square. They bought every house that came onto the market. The neighbours were annoyed as the once peaceful neighbourhood was becoming a trendy party destination in London. Given Benedict's reaction to the family name, Rex remained mum about how often he and Dora had visited the area. Benedict and Dora were on slightly better terms now, and Rex didn't want to be responsible for undoing that.

"Do you have an invitation? How will we get in?"

Rex patted the paper-wrapped whiskey bottle sitting beside him. "This here is the only price of admission."

Benedict glowered at the paper bag as though it was somehow responsible for the Bacchanalian events favoured by the Stracheys.

A line of cars stretching round the corner greeted the men. Rex directed Harris to drop them off. "We'll go ahead on foot. With any luck, we shouldn't be too long. Shall we meet back here in an hour?" Rex checked his watch. "Better make that two, to be safe."

Benedict grumbled under his breath, causing Harris no end of amusement.

"I'll be here, guv. Take your time. I brought a book with me. The gas lamp over there will be enough for me to read." As if to prove his point, Harris pulled the driving blanket across his legs and produced a flask of coffee.

"I'd be better off keeping him company," Benedict said as they walked away. His breath puffed in the wintry air.

Why had Rex brought him along again? When Rex spotted the crowd of people dancing on the pavement in front of Lytton Strachey's home, he remembered. He held out a hand to stop Benedict in his tracks. "Decision time, old chap. If you want to help me identify a killer, slap a smile on your face and do it quick. This is strictly business. I'm not asking you to enjoy yourself, but pretending to have fun will go a long way."

Benedict opened his mouth to argue, but a well-timed glare from Rex had his shoulders rounded in shame. "Quite right,

Rex. I chose to come along. I do mean to help." He stretched his mouth into something vaguely resembling a grin. That was as much as Rex was going to get.

As soon as they made it through the front door of the four-story townhouse, they were immediately sucked into the swirl of activities. Dancing in one room, parlour games in another. It wasn't far off from any other upper class event, if one looked past the scattered trays of drugs and seas of flowing alcohol.

Rex took a cocktail from a passing server and motioned for Benedict to do so as well. While the server was occupied, Rex dumped part of his drink into a planter. Dora had taught him that a half-full glass invited fewer questions.

Sweat ran down Rex's back, and only part of it was due to stress. The heat was stifling thanks to the abundance of people, fireplaces, and radiators. Having missed seeing Rex's trick, Benedict took a generous gulp from the cold drink. Instant regret crossed his face as the heavy pour burned its way down his throat.

"Easy there, mate," Rex chided. These events were much more fun when he wasn't on business and had Dora at his side. Tonight, he wanted to get in and out as fast as possible.

Rex suggested they split up to search for any sign of Rupert. "Keep your wits about you. No more drinks and certainly nothing harder."

Benedict scowled at the suggestion before striding away without a backward glance.

An hour later, they regrouped. Neither had good news. There was no sign of Rupert. No one had seen him. Worse yet, no one was expecting him.

Rex spotted a familiar face coming in the door. It was Nancy Mitford. She always had her finger on the pulse. Rex asked her if she knew where they might find Rupert.

She wrinkled her nose. "Certainly not here. You've got the wrong Strachey. Try James's house. He's hosting a card game."

She swanned off, leaving Rex and Benedict to discuss what to do.

"A card game sounds like a much more intimate event. How will we explain our presence? We can hardly show up empty-handed and uninvited."

Rex searched the room for inspiration and was delighted to see the solution walk through the front door. "Lord Edmund, old chap, fancy seeing you here!"

The lanky, well-dressed man squinted his eyes, as though that would somehow make it easier for his drunken gaze to identify the speaker.

"It's me, Rex." Rex threw an arm over his friend's shoulder. "Nancy Mitford was asking about you. She said something about dancing the foxtrot..." Rex swiped the bottle of wine from Lord Edmund's hand. "I'll add this to the stockpile while you track her down. Off you go!" He nudged the man into the next room. Lord Edmund was too zozzled to question any of it.

Rex held up the bottle for Benedict to see. "We're no longer empty-handed. It's your turn to think of a way to get us inside. Card games are more your bailiwick."

They walked in silence around the private garden that occupied the centre of the square, both grateful for the fresh air and relative quiet. When they reached the other Strachey home, Benedict ran into an old school chum heading in. They followed the man through the door, giving every appearance of being expected.

The scene at this home was much calmer and much more masculine. Not that there weren't any women. It's more that those who were there were all dressed as men.

Despite Rex's expectations, Benedict was out of his

element. Rex had seen Dora don so many costumes. He didn't notice until Benedict made a comment under his breath.

There was no time to explain. Rex spotted Rupert playing cards at one of the tables. They worked their way around the room, socialising until space opened up. Rex claimed the empty seat. One hand later, and another gentleman bowed out, allowing Benedict to join.

The banknotes and coins added up to a valuable pot, but the mood at the table wasn't serious. As Clark had said, the wins and losses ebbed and flowed each week until hardly anyone bothered to keep track. Only the irregular guests like Rex and Benedict carried any real risk of ending up the poorer. Rex made sure to lose a few hands. It was an excellent way to ensure you were encouraged to stay.

Rex surreptitiously studied Rupert. The man's barrel-chest was far less noticeable when seated. He'd been a formidable foe at the front lines, his courage renowned. He'd taken a shot to the leg while rescuing a downed man. If he resented having to depend upon the cane at his side, he didn't show it. There was nothing frail about the man.

Rex studied Rupert's face and body language, searching for any tells. Did scratching his nose mean anything? Rex couldn't spot an obvious pattern.

What a disappointment. Such info would have been useful when Rex began his subtle questioning. Nonetheless, he forged ahead. When the conversation moved on to current events, he took the opportunity to raise the matter of the royal engagement.

"Where's his royal highness this evening? Isn't he a close friend of yours, Rupert? I'd have thought Prince Bertie would be ready for a boy's night after all those balls and tea parties."

The gentleman seated across from Rex guffawed. "Prince

Bertie dares not do anything for fear Lady Elizabeth might change her mind."

Around the table, heads nodded. Only Rupert abstained. He chuckled darkly. "Fear not, Lord Rex. Bertie has had his fun."

"Bertie as in Prince Albert? Surely you jest. The man is as straight as his brother is slanted."

Rupert gave him a sly grin. "Yet they share the same family tree."

"You can hardly make such a bold statement and leave it at that."

"Rupert's bluffing, both with his cards and his words," said James Strachey. He called for the men to show their hands.

If it had been anyone but the host, Rex would have wrung his neck for cutting off the conversation.

Fortunately, the game broke up and everyone rose to stretch their legs. When Rupert headed out the front door, Rex followed. He waved for Benedict to remain behind.

Rupert crossed the street to the private garden. He fumbled in his pocket for a light. Rex came to his rescue.

"A favour for a favour," he proposed, holding the lighter aloft.

Rupert agreed.

"What did you mean by your earlier remark?"

"Are you asking out of curiosity or because you are helping Lord Clark mount a defence?"

"Both," Rex said, answering honestly. "Everyone knows Lord Clark would have made good on the IOU. There was no reason for him to kill Hugh."

"Perhaps, but that is a matter for Scotland Yard to confirm." He took a drag of the cigarette and blew smoke into the air. "Still, I did agree to the trade. There is one person capable of getting Bertie to shrug off his introverted ways. His older brother. "

"Prince Edward?" Rex was thrown off guard. "Edward wants to stop his brother's wedding?"

Rupert pulled a face. "What? That's not what I meant. I doubt he's given Bertie or Elizabeth a second thought. I'm talking about something earlier, around a year or so ago."

Rex searched his memory for any toehold. He had never heard even a hint of a rumour of bad behaviour. Yet Rupert was very confident.

Something happened... but not here. Not in London. Where else had Bertie been?

"The Australian trip," he said.

Rupert nodded, looking impressed. "Exactly. Where better to explore the darker side of life than in the land of our former penal colony? No one there is fit to judge."

"Glass houses," Rex agreed. "Well, go on. You can't leave me hanging now."

"I won't go into the details, as my debt of gratitude for the light isn't that great. Suffice it to say that Bertie infringed upon another man's lands, if you catch my drift."

Rex caught it indeed. An affair with a married woman.

"Edward arranged this? How?"

"Even a blind man could see their attraction. Edward and I lured the man away for a long day of golf. I can't state for a fact what happened in our absence, but I have a good guess." He wiggled his eyebrows and smirked.

Rex smoked his cigarette and contemplated the implications. "Is that why you were against Bertie's engagement? Don't try to deny it. Lord Thomas confessed as much to Theodora."

"I can't say I blame him. If Miss Laurent fluttered her lashes my way, I'd answer whatever she asked."

Rex fought a rush of jealousy, but couldn't keep it off his face.

Rupert laughed again and slapped him on the back. "You've outlasted every other man, Lord Rex. I'd say her attentions are safe."

"Then let us speak of the engagement. My question stands."

Rupert gave a heavy sigh at Rex's insistence on sticking to the topic. "Look, old chap. Bertie isn't like you or I, no matter how close our friendship appears. He has a duty to marry for gain - the Kingdom's gain, that is. I'm sure Sweden or Belgium has a princess they can spare."

"What of his feelings for Elizabeth? They seem true enough. You helped him before. Why not now?"

"If Bertie wished to consort with Elizabeth unofficially, I'd roll out the red carpet. But he refused to even consider it."

Rupert took a final puff of his cigarette and tossed the butt onto the gravelled path. He stamped out the embers and then returned to the fête.

Rex let him leave. His inquiry was equally at an end.

But Rex couldn't help but admire Bertie even more. The man stood against his friends, pursuing his heart's desire.

Would that Rex could do the same.

The topic of marriage still weighed on his mind after Harris collected him from the event. On the drive home, Rex asked Harris why he and Inga had never married.

"I've got the same problem as Dora — what name to list on the marriage banns. Legally, she is still Dorothy Cavendish. But if Lord Rex were to announce his engagement with the missing Cavendish daughter, raised eyebrows would be the least of our problems. As far as everyone in my past life is concerned, I sailed for the States to spend my retirement in warmer climes. Harris sprung from the ashes. Who would marry Inga? A man purported to be on foreign shores or this fake moniker I adopted?" He shrugged. "Inga and I accepted this long ago. We live as man and wife even if the law doesn't recognise us as such."

And so it was for Rex and Dora. He'd never tell anyone, but deep inside, he envied Bertie and Elizabeth.

Chapter 16
The Unexpected Guest

The faint rap on the front door caught Dora's attention as she walked past. Without a second thought, she spun around and opened it.

It was hard to say who was more surprised – Dora at finding Lady FitzClarence standing on her doorstep, or Tabitha at being greeted by the lady of the house.

"Is this a bad time?" Tabitha asked in a halting tone, still unsure which one of them was more out of place.

"Of course not," Dora replied. The other woman's soft tone jostled her out of her stupor. "Where are my manners? Come in and get out of the cold."

Basel, one of the identical twin footmen, appeared at Dora's elbow and took Tabitha's coat and hat.

"My butler is out with Lord Rex at the moment," Dora explained, as though such occurrences happened daily. They did... in Dora's household. But Dora was willing to bet neither Lord Hugh nor Lord Thomas had ever gone gallivanting about town with their butlers. Therefore, Dora made no further attempt to explain or apologise. Such idiosyncrasies were part of her carefully studied allure.

"I hope I'm not intruding," Tabitha said as Dora guided her to the nearby drawing room. "Once I got the idea in my head, I acted fast before I lost my mettle."

"Not at all," Dora replied, brushing aside Tabitha's concern. "Inga and I are passing a quiet afternoon at home. You are welcome to join us. Let me introduce you to her, as I don't believe you've met."

Inga was inside the room, sitting in her favourite chair with a much-inked copy of the day's crossword in her hands. She set the broadsheet aside and wiped the newsprint from her hands with a handkerchief before rising.

"Tabitha, this is Miss Inga Kay, my dear friend and companion of many years."

Inga nodded her head in welcome, keeping a careful distance to avoid offending their titled guest.

Tabitha, however, decided today wasn't the time to stand on ceremony. She crossed the room and offered Inga her hand. "The pleasure is mine. Might I call you Inga, as Theodora does? I find her friendly manner to be a refreshing change after the restrictions of polite society."

"What a fabulous suggestion," Dora said, leaping in. "Please, sit here on the divan. It's close enough to the fire to warm you." Dora took her usual seat on the nearby chair and rang for the housemaid. Cynthia took her time arriving to keep from giving away the fact she'd been eavesdropping at the drawing-room door. "Could you bring tea and a plate of Cook's latest batch of biscuits? Was it ginger you preferred?" Dora asked, glancing at Tabitha.

"If that isn't too much trouble. I've found them helpful in settling my nerves of late."

The women made small talk about the weather until they all had a fresh cup of tea and a plate of biscuits. Then Dora got down to business.

"Not that your visit is in any way unwelcome, but I would be remiss if I didn't ask whether you came with a specific purpose in mind."

Tabitha took a fortifying sip of tea at Dora's bold question. In her widow's weeds, she was even more wan than her usual porcelain complexion. Her carriage, however, remained as upright as ever. "I thought to ask whether you had any updates."

Despite Tabitha's deceptively light tone, Dora had a suspicion that asking for an update wasn't the only reason for the visit. Such a question could be easily posed over the telephone. Tabitha had something more in mind, but what?

Dora studied the woman's face, looking for some hint, but Tabitha was too much of an expert at hiding her true sentiments to reveal anything. As frustrating as it made life now, Dora admired Tabitha's abilities, nonetheless.

Dora set her tea aside and answered Tabitha's question. "There's very little to share, I'm afraid. Rex spoke with Rupert yesterday evening, but nothing he learned indicated Rupert had a motive to kill. Our suspects have been forthcoming about their position against the royal engagement."

"I see."

"Fear not," Inga said, speaking up unexpectedly. She softened her gaze and gave the widow a gentle smile. "Theodora is remarkably skilled at getting what she wants, no matter how impossible the task is. The murderer is out there. Theodora will find him."

Tabitha's shoulders rose, as though a weight had been lifted. She chewed on her lip before finally voicing her real reason for paying a call. "Thank you for your forthrightness. Might I speak as frankly?"

"Of course," Inga replied while Dora looked on. "As you can see, we don't mince words in our home."

"Asking for the update wasn't the only reason for my visit."

Tabitha angled in her chair to face Dora. "I must confess, I'm curious to learn more about how you live."

"How I live?" Dora pretended not to understand. "Barring a few differences, my life is not so dissimilar to yours. As you can see, I live in a comfortable home, with servants to see to my needs. Our social circles even overlap."

While this was strictly true, it was hardly the whole story. Dora kept her full focus on Tabitha to avoid meeting Inga's gaze. She didn't need to see her face to imagine her friend fighting a losing battle against her amusement. It wasn't as though she had another choice. She couldn't mention the morning workouts, lock-picking practice, or political debates to Tabitha.

Tabitha wasn't asking about those things, anyway. Like everyone else, she had no idea about Dora's extracurricular activities. What she wanted to know about was life as an unattached society darling.

Now that she'd broached the topic, Tabitha wasn't willing to be fobbed off with a quick response. She'd got up her courage and meant to carry on. After setting her cup and saucer on a nearby table, she wandered closer to the fire. "Who chose your artwork, Theodora?"

"Some were gifts. Some I chose. For the most part, they are things I've collected during my travels."

"And who decides where you go?"

The needs of the British Empire... Dora couldn't say that. "What can I say? I follow my heart wherever it leads. Now, it wants to stay in London with my darling Rex."

Tabitha gave a longing sigh and sank onto the divan. "That is what I wish to learn from you... from you both," she added, glancing between Dora and Inga. "I am alone now. I'd do anything to change that, but I've come to realise I must accept my newfound, albeit unwelcome, status as a widow. I've seen what happens to other women like me. They rusticate to the countryside or rush into a marriage – anything to avoid facing the reality of being on their own. I thought of you and wondered if there might be a third path available. Following my heart, as you say. But I have no idea where to even start."

Dora understood. She didn't need Tabitha to explain herself further or offer more justifications. In fact, Dora comprehended the situation far better than the other woman could ever imagine. That didn't mean Dora knew what to say in reply.

Dora had been much younger when she'd made the decision to throw off the yoke of society. She'd done so during a period of great international upheaval. Volunteering at the war front or using the cover of a marriage of convenience weren't exactly options.

Sensing her friend's difficulty, Inga poured them all a fresh cup of tea and then dispensed with her own brilliance. "If you want to know more about us, you have only to look around you. Everything here is a reflection of Theodora's desires, and to a lesser extent, also my own. Every painting and antique, furniture and carpet, speaks to our journey from where our lives began to here. However, I must caution you. Studying our choices won't help you find the answer you seek."

"Why?"

"Because the answer to the question of what you, Lady Tabitha FitzClarence, want does not lie within the four walls of this abode. It isn't in your London mansion, nor your country estate. You must search in here," Inga said, tapping her breast. "And you must be patient. The heart speaks when all else is quiet."

Tabitha wrung her hands. "I can't afford to be patient. If I don't act fast, my brother will step in and make all my decisions. Already he has begun making moves. He'll have me packed and living back with our mother and father if I'm not careful."

"Chin up," Dora said. "Perhaps you can convince him to

arrange another marriage for you. He brought Hugh to you. He can't be all that bad at finding someone you'll like."

Tabitha wrinkled her lips. "He deserves little credit for my wedding to Hugh. Do you know, when we were still in the nursery, I made him pretend to be Edward, so I could marry a prince."

"Not Bertie?"

"Oh no," Tabitha said with a laugh. "He's always been far too reserved for my tastes. Edward seemed a good choice until he grew up and went off the rails. That was when I decided to look elsewhere."

"How did you land on Hugh?" Inga asked.

"Desperation? My mother had her eye on every eligible bachelor in London. My father was more focused on their family connections. I didn't dare hope for love... but friendship? That seemed within reach.

"Hugh was still single. We'd exchanged a few letters during the war years. When he came home, we carried on. All innocent," she hastened to add. "Favourite books, a shared love of the opera, that sort of thing. I worked up my courage and floated the idea one day while we were out for a walk. His parents were hounding on him to settle down. Better the devil you know, and all that. To my great relief, he said he thought it was a capital solution. Hardly romantic, but it is a better tale than many in my set have to tell."

"Eventually, your heart caught up with your head," Dora reminded her in a soft tone. "I don't think you need our help, Tabitha. You simply need to trust yourself again, as you did before. You'll find a way."

"Let's hope... but this time around, I wouldn't say no to a head start."

Tabitha stayed for another hour, asking question after

question as Dora showed her around the public rooms of the house. She was more interested in the stories behind Dora's purchases than their provenance. When she left, it was with a smile on her face and a promise to visit again soon.

"Poor Tabitha. She was done in, improved outlook notwithstanding. Let us both hope she gets more rest in the coming days," Inga said.

"I imagine her nights are long, but I suspect grief isn't the only reason for her exhaustion." Dora patted her midsection. "Stomach trouble, ginger biscuits, and fatigue point to the possibility of another condition."

"Do you think she knows?"

Dora shrugged. "If she does, she hasn't told anyone. But it would explain why Hugh insisted on checking the room before she met with Bertie. After their earlier loss, he'd have taken great care to keep her calm and safe."

Inga agreed. They returned to the drawing room and retrieved the newspaper and magazine they'd set aside when their visitor had arrived. After a few minutes, Dora caught Inga staring off into space.

"Trouble with one of the crossword clues?"

"What?" Inga shook off her thoughts. "Err, no. Wool-gathering, that's all." Inga lowered her gaze to the crossword and made a mark with her pen.

Dora knew her friend too well to buy the explanation. Inga didn't wool-gather. It wasn't in her nature. If she was lost in thought, there had to be a reason. Dora had an idea what it might be, but she was almost afraid to ask. She bucked up her courage.

"Do you... ahem, I mean did you..."

"Spit it out, Dorothy," Inga chided without lifting her gaze from the paper.

"Do you want children? Someday, I mean. You're still young. We both are."

Inga penned another word in the line of squares. "I already have a child."

Dora's mouth dropped open wide enough for flies to go in. "You do? Since when?!"

Inga lifted her gaze and smirked at Dora. "Since about five years ago, when a certain debutante on the run asked me to stand in as her mother."

"Hardy har har." Dora rolled her eyes at her dear friend's saucy reply. The cheek! It did, however, give her the courage to speak directly. "I meant a baby. With Harris."

"Since you've asked, I'll tell you that the question is irrelevant. Harris and I made our choices to enter these lives with open eyes. We wanted to be together, even if it meant Harris leaving behind his past identity to assume a false name and role as a butler. It didn't matter then, and it doesn't matter now that we can't marry under fake names.

"As for the other, we share the same opinion with regard to children. Despite how often we thumb our noses at convention, neither of us is keen to have a child that the rest of the world would deem as illegitimate."

The threat of tears made Dora's eyes burn. Despite Inga's blasé attitude, she still felt guilty. "I'm sorry for my part in restricting your life choices."

Inga sat up at Dora's despondent tone. She set her paper and pen aside again and offered her hand to Dora. "You have nothing for which to apologise. Not a one of us is held here by force. Every morning, we make the decision to stay. Yes, that choice has consequences. Trust me, dear Dora, we make the choice with open eyes."

Inga was right, of course, but that didn't stop Dora from contemplating what might be. Like their current investigation, every step opened up new pathways for exploration. As long as Dora had breath in her chest and blood moving in her veins, she'd keep going forward. To the identity of the killer... and perhaps even beyond.

She'd long since decided that when it came to her future, nothing was outside the realm of possibility.

Chapter 17
The Ultimatum

R ex was at his grandmother's home, having decamped to her library for the afternoon. He and Dora had exhausted their list of suspects. Either they'd missed something during their interviews, or they were on the wrong track. Rex had turned to his grandmother's vast store of gossip for inspiration.

As always, his grandmother was highly pleased to be of assistance. She also wasn't alone. Sitting with them was none other than the Duchess of Dorset, also known as Dora's mother. Like Benedict, Lady Adaline Cavendish wasn't prepared to sit on the sidelines while her daughter did all the hard work.

There was nothing unusual about the two titled women spending time together. Edith had been one of the first women to welcome Adaline into the upper set following her marriage to Dora's father. Coming from America, Adaline couldn't depend upon school friends and family members to fill her social calendar. Many had looked upon the so-called Dollar Princesses with disdain, as the wealthy young women used their dowries to procure titles and pedigree.

Edith had recognised that Adaline wasn't like the rest of

that pack. She'd married for love. The Duke of Dorset had no need for funds for his bank accounts. He'd been free to pick whomever he wanted, and it was no one else's business if he chose a beauty from the other side of the pond.

Was it any wonder that Lady Adaline wanted to offer her support to Bertie and Elizabeth? She, more than most, would understand what it was like to be judged unfairly due to the circumstances of her birth. Knowing why she was there convinced Rex to avail himself of her offer.

Dora's mother set her teacup aside and gave Rex her full attention. "To recap, Bertie snubbed his nose at the official list of brides and chased after Lady Elizabeth until she said yes. Three of his four closest friends felt he was making a grave mistake. Only Hugh stood apart."

"And Tabitha," Rex added.

"Indeed. Tabitha asked Audley to arrange a private word via anonymous letters. Hugh preceded her to the meeting space. Someone else joined him. They spoke, and then the other person stabbed Hugh through the heart. From this, you presume the suspect must be one of Bertie's closest friends. Have I got that right?"

"Yes, that covers it. Thomas, Nicholas, and Rupert knew Hugh didn't support their plans to halt the wedding. They were all there on the night in question. If they had even a hint that Hugh intended to tell Bertie of their plans, any one of them might have acted."

"Thus far, however," his grandmother said, cutting into the conversation, "none of them is keeping their thoughts on the marriage a secret. They don't seem particularly worried about this getting back to Bertie. So, where's the motive to kill?"

Rex ran his hand through his hair and heaved a deep sigh. "I don't know. That's why I'm here. What if Dora and I are on the wrong track? What if this has nothing to do with the letters or why we were at the party? Have you learned anything about Hugh that might be of value to us?"

Edith motioned for Lady Adaline to go first.

"I looked into Hugh's household. The only bit of gossip I could find is that the housekeeper fired a staff member three weeks ago. Caught her stealing the silver, from what I heard."

In such a case, the fired staff would have had greater reason to take action against the housekeeper. Rex stopped himself from dismissing it out of hand. "Could the staff member have found a position at Windsor?"

"Definitely not. It was a below-stairs maid. Even if she somehow talked her way into the castle, she'd have stuck out like a sore thumb at the engagement ball."

"Grandmama, please tell me you have something," Rex begged.

"I doubt it is of any greater use. In addition to your Lord Clark, there were two other men who lost money to Hugh at that card game. I wasn't able to find out whether either of them repaid the IOUs, nor whether the sums were great enough to cause them pain. I've got their names here." She pulled a slip of paper from her pocket and handed it over.

Rex skimmed the names, recognising them both. Neither of the men seemed any more likely to kill over a debt than Clark did. Rex was considering his next course of action when the telephone trilled. As he was closest, he answered the call.

"Bankes-Fernsby, here," he said, accustomed to naming himself when he answered Dora's phone.

"Miss Laurent was right about where I'd find you. Consider this a courtesy call. DCI Miller is on his way to Lord Audley's. You have fifteen minutes to get there."

The caller hung up without another word. It was no matter. Rex had recognised the voice. After all, he'd spoken to Rupert the night before.

Rex debated phoning Dora, but there was no point. She'd never make it across town in the limited time frame available. He'd update her later. She'd understand.

"Bad news?" his grandmother asked after catching sight of his frown.

"I'm not sure. Apologies, but I must run. Something urgent has come up that needs my attention."

Lady Edith and Lady Adaline waved him off, promising to keep at their task. If there was a stone left, they'd turn it over.

Rather than wasting time bringing the car around, Rex chose to walk. According to his watch, he'd arrived with three minutes to spare. Lord Audley's butler caught sight of Rex's tense shoulders and worry lines and got out of his way, pointing in the direction of the drawing room. Lord Audley was inside, reading the paper. He set it aside when Rex walked in.

"DCI Miller is on his way," Rex announced without even a hello. Without asking permission, he instructed the footman to find Lord Clark. "Any idea what this is about?"

"None. But let me handle it, whatever it is."

Rex had no problems agreeing to that.

The doorbell rang as Clark entered the drawing room. Lord Audley's butler waited until all three men were seated before answering the door.

Despite the minimal notice, they'd managed to set up an impressive tableau. Rex sat on a leather sofa. Clark was in a heavy Georgian wooden chair with Audley standing behind him.

DCI Miller strode into the drawing room, but stopped once he got a look at the scene.

Once again, Lord Audley did not invite him to take a seat.

Rupert came in after him, having slowed long enough to pass his coat and hat to the footman. He didn't wait for an invitation, but helped himself to a chair close to the door. He wasn't exactly aligning himself with the Detective, but he wasn't disowning him either.

At the raised eyebrows, he explained, "Prince Albert requested I act as a liaison with Scotland Yard, and the detective suggested I join him here."

"I take it there's an update on the investigation?" Audley asked, glancing between Rupert and Miller.

Miller nodded. "We are preparing the paperwork for an arrest."

Rex flinched at the hard edge of the detective's tone. He didn't need to be a mind reader to guess where this was going.

Poor Clark was doing his best to keep his face clear of emotion, but Rex was close enough to see the sweat forming on his brow and the tremble in his hands.

Lord Audley, however, refused to be cowed. He rested a hand on Clark's shoulder. "This is excellent news, as much as I've enjoyed having a houseguest. I'm sure Lord Clark will be greatly relieved to return to his own abode."

"Unfortunately, that is not his destination. The arrest papers will have his name on them. I've brought along several guards to position at the entrances to the house. Out of respect for you, my lord, we won't take him into custody now. We'll arrange a time for you to bring him to the station."

"His royal highness would prefer to keep this from the papers, if at all possible," Rupert added.

"I see...," Audley paused for a moment to gather his thoughts. "Please let Prince Albert know there is a flaw in his plan."

Lord Rupert spluttered, "I beg your pardon."

"Lord Clark is innocent. I have no intentions of sitting quietly while a miscarriage of justice takes place."

Lord Rupert squared his shoulders as if preparing for battle, but DCI Miller staid him with a raised hand. He reached into a pocket and retrieved his notepad.

"I expected you might have questions, so I've prepared notes. Lord Hugh had no known enemies. He did not engage in disreputable activities." Unlike some...he left unsaid, but his glance at Lord Clark conveyed his thoughts.

"I am well aware of Lord Hugh's spotless reputation, detective," Audley said.

"We've interviewed Lord Hugh's family, friends, household...only one motive has come to light." DCI Miller took a breath and then pointed at Clark. "Your unpaid debt."

"But I simply forgot!" Clark exclaimed. "I was foxed that evening. It's the only reason Hugh got the best of me. He was an abysmal card player. Tell him, Rupert."

Rupert gave a wry smile. "He was, indeed. His every thought showed on his face."

Apparently not all of them, Rex thought. Hugh had kept silent on his wife's attempts to thwart the other men's plans to double cross their friend.

Lord Audley spoke again, retaking control of the conversation. "Since you have your notes to hand, let me ask you this, Detective. What did you learn about Lord Clark's financial state?"

Miller grimaced. "We found no issues there."

"What of his past exploits? Knowing what little I do of his entertainment preferences, I can't imagine this is his first IOU."

"It is not," Miller admitted. "But that doesn't get around the fact that Lord Clark was found standing over the body with the murder weapon in hand."

"I received a note! I thought to help him! I was flummoxed by the blood."

"Perhaps," Miller said in a cold tone, "or maybe you wrote the note to use in case you were caught. There are, quite simply, no other possible suspects. I have no choice but to proceed with the evidence I have to hand. That evidence points to you."

Rex saw Lord Audley's fingers tighten on Clark's shoulder.

"DCI Miller, it would be a shame to mar your excellent record by arresting an innocent man. I encourage you to think carefully before you do something you will regret."

"Are you threatening me?" Miller asked, getting his back up.

"Not at all. If anything, this is a warning for Rupert to pass along to his highness. If Prince Albert wishes his engagement to proceed with no more negative publicity, he must be one-hundred-per cent confident that you have caught the right man."

"I'm sorry, my lord, but there is no further line of investigation available to us." He tucked his notepad back into his coat and opened his hands wide. "If you have knowledge of any evidence or suspects we should consider, send word. Otherwise, we will expect Lord Clark at the station tomorrow. I'll ring later with the exact time."

DCI Miller showed himself out. Rupert, however, didn't follow.

"Does his royal highness have another message for us?"

"No, this one is from me. I am not unsympathetic about your position. The engagement is putting an unnecessary strain on the timings. If you want to help Lord Clark, advise Bertie to delay his nuptials."

Rex had sat silently until now, but Rupert's casual disregard for his friend's marriage rubbed him the wrong way.

"Why are you so quick to sacrifice Bertie's happiness?"

"Bertie will be happy only if he does what is best for the crown. He can't see that now, but I can. All his friends can."

Except Hugh, that is. But Hugh wasn't there to speak his mind.

Audley coughed to get everyone's attention. "My dedication

to crown and country is well known. I don't see any reason for Bertie and Elizabeth's marriage not to proceed. Despite my warning, it is not my aim to disrupt their nuptials. For their sake, for all our sake, I hope we identify the real killer soon."

"On that, at least, we are all in agreement. Including DCI Miller and the rest of Scotland Yard." Rupert rose and made his goodbyes.

After he left, Clark slumped in his seat. All the energy fled his body, leaving only worry and dread behind. "What am I going to do?" he moaned.

"Nothing," Audley said in a voice that left no room for nonsense. "You must have faith in Rex and Theodora. They solved Freddy's killer and unmasked a murderous jewel thief."

Clark looked at Rex and pleaded, "Can you do this?"

Rex dug deep, displaying a confidence he didn't feel. He had to do so, for Clark's sake. "We can — Dora and I will save you from a life behind bars."

Rex didn't dare let any of his fear and doubt show in his voice. Inside, however, his spirit trembled. Their investigation had hit the same brick wall as DCI Miller's. He and Dora would have to find a way to push through it.

Chapter 18
Windsor, Again?

The investigation had reached the point that Rex and Dora needed space to spread out and review their findings thus far. For times like this, Dora's secret study was their preferred choice. Rex paced back and forth along the length of the room. He'd come home from Lord Audley's determined to solve the crime. It was the how that had him stumped.

"If you keep that up, you're going to wear a hole in my carpet," Dora chastised Rex. "While I know you can afford a replacement, this particular one will be difficult to source, seeing as how I bought it from a market in Egypt."

Rex flopped into the nearest chair, but did no better at staying still. His nervous energy was fast becoming contagious. Dora wasn't one to crumble under stress, but seeing Rex tug on his shirt collar was having an effect.

He'd been that way since he'd returned from Lord Audley's with the news that Clark was to be arrested. "I'm sorry, Dora. I know I'm not being much help. If you'd seen Clark today, you'd understand my stress. I promised we'd clear his name."

Dora was no stranger to the pressure that felt like a stranglehold around your neck. The difference was she had enough experience to know how to ignore it. It was a task easier said than done. Rex would master the skill over time, but telling him that wasn't going to help. Instead, she set her pen down on the sheet of butcher paper covering her coffee table, and rose to give Rex a hug.

She settled into his lap and wrapped her arms around his neck. As the warmth from her body seeped into his, his heartbeat slowed and his breathing evened out. "We're banging our heads against the proverbial wall, but that isn't necessarily a bad thing."

"What do you mean?"

Instead of answering his question, Dora got up to fetch a book from her shelf. "Here. Open this to the page I have bookmarked."

"How They Succeeded?" Rex furrowed his brow as he glanced at the title, but did as she asked. There was a single line of text underlined on the page. He read it aloud. "*I do not think that there is any other quality so essential to success of any kind as the quality of perseverance. It overcomes almost everything, even nature.*"

"I picked up that book from a secondhand shop in Paris, thinking I might find some useful advice. That particular quote stuck with me. It's from John D. Rockefeller, one of the great American success stories. Whenever I hit a blind alley, I pull that book out and reread that line."

Dora took the book back and replaced it on the shelf. "While you were pacing, I made some notes." She pointed at the butcher paper. It was covered with scribbled names in circles, connected to one another by a series of lines. "This whole time, we've had Hugh at the centre of our research. That's where we went wrong."

Rex shifted position to give himself a better view of her

notes. He traced the lines, mumbling under his breath, before turning to her. "What am I missing?"

"We were both missing the obvious." Dora returned to her seat, picked up her pen, and scratched Hugh's name from the paper. Out to the side, she wrote another.

"Prince Bertie?" Rex sucked in a breath. "Of course! The main crime isn't who killed Hugh, but who is so determined to stop Bertie's marriage that they'd kill to get their way."

"Exactly. You and I are experts at interpreting body language. We need to see how our suspects act when they are with Bertie and Elizabeth. Do any of them make snide remarks? Are they glaring daggers when Bertie isn't looking? That sort of thing."

"That's brilliant. I agree completely, but how are we going to do that before tomorrow afternoon?"

"I won't know the answer to that until I check Prince Bertie's official schedule. Lord Audley had it couriered over in case it might come in handy. Let me grab it." Dora shuffled through papers on her desk until she found the page in question. "The gods are smiling upon us, Rex, although I'll warn you we'll have a very early start."

"Go on..."

"First thing in the morning, Bertie has a standing appointment for his weekly ride through Windsor Great Park. I overheard someone talking about it during the engagement party. A very intimate event, attended only by Bertie, Elizabeth, and Bertie's closest friends."

"And us," Rex added. "Shall I ring Audley and see if he can arrange an invitation?"

Dora stopped him before he could head for the telephone. "You'll need to make some calls, but there's no need to ask Audley for help. I don't want to give any of them warning. To do that, we're going to have to invite ourselves. "

* * *

Rex required only one telephone call to make the arrangements. His boyhood school sat within spitting distance of the castle grounds. The headmaster was only too willing to loan Rex a pair of horses for the morning in exchange for a generous donation to the building fund.

Rex and Dora turned in early, for once, and were on the road to Windsor by daybreak. With the rising sun at their back and flasks of coffee in hand, they lowered the windows of the Rolls-Royce. The crisp air wiped the sleepy cobwebs from their minds.

The college stable master had the horses ready to go. He'd chosen a pair of thoroughbreds, both retired racehorses now used to teach the college boys how to ride. "Solid temperaments, but if you give them a bit of headroom, they'll fly over the ground."

"Just the way I like them. We'll take good care of them," Dora assured the man. He gave her a boost into the saddle and they were off.

Rex led the way, being knowledgeable of the terrain. Dora sat back and enjoyed the view. Despite being on an unfamiliar horse, and a spirited stallion to boot, he was utterly at ease. If she didn't love him already, the sight of his muscular form and his blonde hair glistening in the sun would have tipped her over the edge.

When he informed her they were entering the park grounds, she tamped down her emotions. Now wasn't the time for romantic sentiments. She dug her heels into the horse's flank, and it shot forward. "Catch me if you can," she called out.

Dora didn't need to look back. She had no doubts Rex would keep up.

They raced across the cold ground until they caught sight of the royal party cantering through the park. They were easy enough to recognise. Bertie and Elizabeth rode beside one another. Thomas's black hair and lean form proved him to be the man on Bertie's other side. Rupert and Nicholas brought up the rear, talking to one another.

The royals weren't allowed out alone, even this close to the castle. Four guards accompanied them, two out front and two more lingering back. They were at ease in their saddles, keeping enough distance from the group to give them a modicum of privacy. It was one of the guards who spotted Dora and Rex.

Rex hailed them with a halloo and a wave. Thomas recognised them first and called for the others to wait. Bertie assured the guards all was well.

"Lord Rex, Miss Laurent, we weren't expecting you," Thomas said, eyeing the pair with concern.

"I hope we aren't intruding," Rex replied. "We were in need of a breath of fresh air to clear our minds. We didn't realise anyone else would be out at this hour. I hope we aren't holding you up." Rex inclined his head at Prince Bertie and Lady Elizabeth, making it clear to whom he addressed his words.

"Not at all. There is space aplenty, as you can see. You are welcome to join us for the remainder of the ride." Prince Bertie turned to Lady Elizabeth, almost as an afterthought. "As long as that is fine with you, my darling."

"It will be nice to have another woman along," Elizabeth said quietly. She gave Dora a tentative smile. "You seem very at home in the saddle, Miss Laurent."

"It is hardly a challenge to keep one's seat with a saddle and stirrups. Now, riding bareback across the Sahara...that was much more difficult."

"And certainly a stimulating tale. Will you tell it to me?" This time, Lady Elizabeth's enthusiasm showed no hesitation.

Dora kept her satisfaction to herself. She had heard it had

taken a visit from the Queen herself to convince Elizabeth to say yes. Dora had hedged her bets, judging Elizabeth would appreciate a spirited companion. It seemed she called it correctly.

"Of course, my lady," Dora replied.

"Excellent. We'll stop soon for refreshments. It will be nice to have something else to discuss while the men carry on about the cricket."

With that, they set off.

The undulating hills of the Great Park rolled beneath the group as they kept a steady cadence. The morning fog battled against the sunlight, not yet ready to relinquish its hold.

The riders took turns taking the lead, setting a merry chase through the park grounds.

Dora's blood pumped and her senses awakened.

The frosty air burned her cheeks and sent her bobbed curls bouncing free of their pins. If it had been a real race, her view would have narrowed until all she saw was the ground rolling before her.

But there was no prize today, other than the sheer joy of being alive in the world. For a brief moment, she was free of all encumbrances.

She allowed her gaze to roam across the grounds. From the castle atop the hill to the copse of trees to her right, peace reigned supreme.

Until it didn't.

She was side-by-side with Elizabeth, following the Long Walk leading to the castle proper. Dora heard the crack first. Her move was instinctual, born of her training and brief period working near the front lines.

Dora sprang into action at the same moment as the birds scattered from the treetops. She kicked out with her left foot, while giving a fierce tug on the reins.

Her foot connected with the rear flank of Lady Elizabeth's horse, causing it to veer sideways.

She wasn't sure it would be enough until her own horse stumbled as the bullet skimmed across its neck. It reared in pain.

Dora was still in motion. If she was coming off the horse, better it be on her terms. Her desert riding days had taught her more than how to stay on. She'd learned how to work with the motion, to limit the damage from the inevitable falls.

She hit the grass lawn hard enough to knock the breath out of her. Her tucked roll protected her face and head. She'd be bruised, but otherwise whole.

From the moment she heard the crack of the rifle to the bone-jarring path of her landing, time had moved in slow motion.

It returned to normal speed with stomach-churning quickness. Hoarse shouts and frantic whinnies filled the air.

The guards that had been trailing behind swooped in around the royal couple to usher them to safety.

That left Rex free to rush to Dora's aid. But for a moment, he didn't. His face went white and then, with a shake of his head, he spurred his horse on, racing to Dora's side. With no regard for the risk of an active shooter aiming their way, he slid off his horse and hurried to check on her.

"Are you hurt? Did he hit you?" Rex's panicked gaze roamed over her, searching for any sign of blood.

"No, I'm uninjured. I promise." Dora cupped his chin to calm him. One look at his ashen face made her ask in return, "Are you alright?"

His voice was hoarse with emotion when he explained, "The gunshot triggered another flashback to the war. I saw... no, it's not important. Your cry of alarm pulled me back from the brink. No memory can be more important to me than you are."

Both of them were full of more thoughts and questions, but

this wasn't the time or place for raising them. Already, Rupert and Nicholas were drawing close.

Dora pitched her voice low enough for only Rex to hear.

"We got it wrong again. The target isn't Bertie. It's Elizabeth."

Chapter 19
Time to Come Clean

R ex barely had time to process Dora's statement before
concerned guards swarmed them.

"I'm fine," Dora said repeatedly, not that any of the guards
were listening. They had orders from Prince Bertie to bring her
to the castle for a full medical check.

The castle was exactly where they needed to go, but Dora
had a mulish expression on her face. She hated playing the
damsel in distress.

"Darling, let the doctor look you over," Rex said, cutting off
Dora's attempts to decline. "For my sake."

He wiggled his eyebrows at her and she finally caught on to
his plan. "I'm being silly," she admitted, giving the guard an
apologetic smile. "Must have hit my head harder than I realised."

"Ride with me," Rex said, pulling her toward his steed.
"Although the injury to your horse is minor, we shouldn't tax it
unnecessarily."

Dora's horse snorted in agreement, as though it understood.
Its coat and mane were damp with blood from where the bullet
had grazed its neck.

Rex hugged Dora tight against his chest, needing to feel the breath in her chest as much as to whisper words in her ears. He'd speak with the men. If at all possible, she was to catch up with Lady Elizabeth.

A lady's maid and a footman stood ready at the castle entrance. Rex sized up the situation and decided he didn't want Dora limping along the castle corridors. No matter how many times she reassured him she was hale and hearty, he wasn't taking any chances. He carried her in his arms, following the hurried steps of the lady's maid. The woman said Lady Elizabeth was waiting in her private sitting room and the doctor was on his way.

Rex made sure Dora was comfortable before taking his leave. In all honesty, she appeared to be holding up better than Elizabeth. The bride-to-be was waxen faced, having never been so close to a threat. Did she even realise that the bullet had been aimed her way?

Rex didn't stay to ask. That was Dora's task. His work lay elsewhere.

He assumed the footman would guide him to the men, but instead he was shown into a small antechamber. Prince Bertie was the only one there.

"Miss Laurent?" he asked as soon as Rex came through the door.

"She's in good spirits. Other than scrapes and bruises, she escaped injury."

"Thank god," Prince Bertie sighed. He tossed a glance at the double-doors on the other side of the room. "I'm waiting to speak with my father. I'd prefer he not hear of this from anyone else."

Rex preferred King George not hear of them at all. Lord Audley would be in firm agreement on that point. "There's no need to worry him on our behalf. What's important is we're all safe. For all we know, it might have been a stray shot."

"On the Long Walk?" Bertie was unconvinced. "First Hugh, now this. Until Elizabeth and I announced our engagement, none other than my closest friends found me interesting. The spotlight follows wherever Edward goes. Now, I'd like to fade from view again. I want everyone to be safe."

"We all do." That was all Rex managed to say before the door to the king's study opened. He bowed his head to Bertie and scooted out the other door.

The footman was still there, waiting silently to accede at any royal request. Rex put the man to good use. "Are Lord Thomas, Lord Nicholas, and Rupert still here?"

"Yes, my lord. They're waiting upstairs, in his highness's private quarters. Do you wish to join them?"

"First, I must make a phone call. Is there a private telephone I can use?"

The footman led him to a nearby alcove and then moved far enough away to give Rex some privacy.

Rex's first call was to Lord Audley. He chose his words carefully, never knowing who might be listening in. "Put a stopper in any plans to visit the Yard. We've had an incident here. Everyone is fine, but the situation has most definitely... evolved."

"Understood. I'll look forward to hearing more from you after your return to London."

Rex rang off and then placed a second call, this time to Dora's home. He conveyed a similar message, although this time, he amended the bit about everyone being okay. Instead, he told Harris Theodora had taken a tumble and would need to put her feet up.

Harris bit back a curse and said he would let Miss Kay know the news. Rex was glad he wasn't the one having to tell Inga that Dora was hurt. Inga was worse than a mother bear when Dora came home with a bruise or cut.

His immediate tasks complete, Rex asked the footman to show him to the others. A few minutes later, he entered yet another room. This time, the door revealed a masculine study furnished with heavy wooden furniture. Leather-bound books filled the shelves.

He spotted Nicholas and Thomas first. The men were helping themselves to Bertie's bar cart. Despite the early hour, Nicholas poured generous splashes from a crystal decanter.

Nicholas passed a glass to Rex. "Here, man. My nerves are shot." He flinched and then added, "Poor choice of words."

Rex studied the men's faces over the rim of his drink. They were as shaken as he felt. Thomas's hand trembled when he raised his glass. Nicholas looked sick. Rupert stared out the window as though in search of answers.

There was nothing to be found outside. The shooter was likely long gone, having a sizeable head start on his or her escape.

Rupert should have been looking inside. Rex suspected the answer was in this room, but how should he get the men to talk? He could hardly play dumb. They all knew he and Dora had been asking questions.

They'd tried treading lightly, leaning upon trusted friends, and inviting information-sharing in confidence. This was the result they'd obtained.

It was time for a different approach. Someone was willing to go so far as to plot an assassination attempt. From what he knew, Rex couldn't believe all these men were involved. Valid rationale or not, none of them would be able to justify killing a royal bride. That was a hanging offence.

Yet, one of them had decided to prevent the wedding at all costs. But who?

It was time to set the men against one another. He placed his still full whiskey glass on a nearby table and strode into the centre of the room. He chose his position with great care, making sure he could see all three of the men at the same time.

With his back to the fireplace, Rupert was on his right, gazing out the window. Thomas and Nicholas sat on opposite ends of a long sofa.

Rex cleared his throat to get their attention. "Lord Clark sits under lock and key at Lord Audley's London home, and has been there since the night of the engagement ball. He has no access to the outside world. There is no chance he is behind today's terrible occurrence. So, let us put aside this farce that he is somehow to blame for Hugh's death."

He waited a beat, but no one argued. He had their full attention.

"The three of you made no bones about your opposition to this marriage. Your claims to be acting for the good of the nation no longer stand. Murdering Elizabeth before Bertie's eyes would lead to utter devastation. If any of you know something about what happened this morning, you must come clean. If not to me, then to Lord Audley."

"Of course we know nothing," Thomas spluttered. "Do you think we'd stand idly by as one of us acts in cold blood? My brother-in-law is dead! My sister is a widow!"

Rex hardened his heart against the man's entreaties. "Are you so sure of your friends? Surely you don't believe these events are unrelated. To the best of my knowledge, only three people in this world are actively trying to stop the wedding."

"Were trying," Nicholas whispered. He raised his voice. "With Hugh gone, we set our concerns aside. We came today to show Bertie our support. And to honour Hugh's memory."

Honour? Nicholas spoke far too cavalierly of a word he didn't understand. Rex lost his grip on his fury.

"Someone stabbed Hugh through the heart because he dared to get in your way. I can almost believe it wasn't Thomas.

Was it you, Nicholas? When that wasn't enough, did you arrange for the shooter to be on the castle grounds this morning?"

"Absolutely not!" Nicholas rose from his chair, his fists clenched. Rex widened his stance and prepared to take whatever Nicholas threw his way.

"Stop this!" Thomas leapt to his feet and grabbed Nicholas's arm. "What will Bertie think if he comes in here and finds you two fighting?"

Let him come, Rex thought. Let him see the truth of these men. He raised his hand and pointed at the remaining man. "That leaves you, Rupert."

Rupert turned away from the window to face the room. Sunlight streamed in behind him, making it almost impossible to see the expression on his face.

Rex squinted his eyes. Sun or not, he would see through to this man's soul, if that was what it took.

Rupert spread his fingers wide, searching for balance amidst the tumultuous waves of anger battering the room. There was no mistaking the emotion in his haggard voice. "I have known Elizabeth longer than any of you. I grew up alongside her. I'd no sooner hurt her than my own sister."

"Face it, man," Thomas said, cutting Rex off from further recriminations. "We are as lost as you. There must be something else afoot, but I'll be damned if I can tell you what it is."

Nicholas and Rupert added their agreement, sharing Thomas's consternation with the terrible situation.

Rex would get nothing more from them. Prince Bertie arrived soon after and the discussion turned to the topic of keeping Elizabeth safe.

Prince Bertie showed no signs of distrust in his friends. This was why Lord Audley had held off telling the Prince what was really going on. Living under the watchful eye of the nation was bad enough. Bertie needed his confidants.

Rex wouldn't tear them from him until he knew for certain who was to blame. No matter what they claimed, Rex remained convinced that the culprit sat in this room.

Too bad he had no idea who it might be.

Chapter 20
A Lady's Confession

In Lady Elizabeth's sitting room, Dora gripped onto the edge of the sofa cushion to keep from strangling the doctor. She was a terrible patient at the best of times. It took all her control not to snap at the doctor as he continued to chastise her in a patronising tone.

She'd known she was in trouble the moment he walked through the door. Dr McIntyre wore a trim suit and a supercilious attitude. He'd shown Lady Elizabeth the proper obeisance due to the fiancee of a royal heir. When Elizabeth introduced him to Miss Laurent, sans title or other honorific, he'd curled his lip in disdain.

Of course, with Lady Elizabeth by her side, there was a limit to how far the good doctor could go. He walked right to the edge of the line. For example, while checking her pulse, he asked whether Lady Elizabeth was suffering from stress. When he listened to her lungs, he remarked positively upon the breadth of Elizabeth's hips. It was a good thing Dora wasn't badly injured, as the man didn't listen to a word she said.

Dora might have been his current patient. Elizabeth,

however, was his route to royal recognition. If Dora didn't put a stop to his relentless sucking up, she'd never learn a thing.

She gritted her teeth and forced the doctor to back up enough to allow her to put her feet on the ground. "I appreciate your time and care, Dr McIntyre, but I'm sure you have other patients who have greater need than I."

Dr McIntyre preened under her compliments. Still, it wouldn't do for him to leave without making one last attempt to put her in her place. "You are very lucky you didn't break your neck, Madam. In the future, stick to more docile mounts," he said, wagging his finger at her.

Dora clenched her teeth to keep from biting his head off. Even the most placid mount in the world would take umbrage at a bullet grazing its head. There was no point in defending or justifying her actions. This old fuddy duddy, in his glasses and stiff wool suit, would never believe she'd known what she was doing. If anything, he'd examine her head again for signs of injury.

"I'm sure Miss Laurent will take greater care in the future," Lady Elizabeth said in a well-timed intervention. "I'll see that she rests. You can leave her with me."

"That's right in line with my prescription, my lady. Rest, a warm bath before bed, and two spoonfuls of this," he said, reaching for his bag. "To calm the nerves."

"My nerves are fine," Dora snapped. She stopped herself from saying more by taking a deep breath. Her ribs twinged, but she didn't let the pain show on her face. "All I need is a fortifying cup of your English tea and I' ll be... how do you say?" She thickened her fake accent. "Good as rain?"

"Right as rain," Lady Elizabeth supplied. "Tea is on the way. " She turned to the footman stationed nearest the door. "Please show Dr McIntyre the way out."

Lady Elizabeth had certainly mastered the imperious tone

of a royal. Dora admired her even more for it. Royal life would eat up the weak-willed. Lady Elizabeth had gumption.

The doctor pointed again at the small bottle of laudanum before taking his leave. Dora didn't relax until the door closed behind him.

Elizabeth rested her hand on her forehead and dropped into the nearest chair. "I'll have to make a note to find my own doctor before Bertie and I have children. Can you imagine how he must treat his pregnant patients? He'd have me on bedrest for nine months."

"Perish the thought," Dora muttered. "Pass me that bottle."

Elizabeth's brow wrinkled in confusion, but she handed the laudanum over as requested. Dora twisted the cap, leaned over, and poured a measure into the potted Areca palm sitting beside her. "If the doctor comes back to check, you can reassure him with all honesty that you saw me help myself to a dose."

Elizabeth snorted and then covered her face in embarrassment. Her shoulders shook with silent laughter until she got a hold of herself. "You must think me a fool for laughing at a time like this."

"I think you human, Lady Elizabeth. While a rare trait for those of the royal persuasion, it isn't a weakness."

Dora's earnest expression underscored the honesty of her answer. Elizabeth's mouth opened in surprise, but she recovered soon enough. She settled into her chair and fixed Dora in her gaze. "Are you certain you're all right, Miss Laurent?"

"I have a few bumps and bruises, but they are nothing compared to what might have happened had I not acted as quickly as I did. Bruises are easily healed with a treatment of my companion's special arnica paste. A gunshot wound would be a much greater challenge to repair."

Assuming the victim wasn't dead...

Dora didn't need to say the words out loud. Elizabeth was wise enough to grasp the seriousness of what had happened.

"Do you think they were aiming at me?" Elizabeth held up a hand to stave off a reply. "Of course they were. I don't understand what is happening. They first killed Hugh. Now I'm in their sights. These events must be connected, but I cannot see how."

Dora held her tongue while she studied the future princess's body language. There was no hint of guile in her expression, nor in the tense set of her shoulders. Lady Elizabeth sat like a terrified fisherman, rocking in a rowboat while the storms grew ever more fierce.

There was no point pretending the dark clouds didn't exist. The best way to protect Elizabeth was to make it clear that the danger was not imaginary.

"There is something you should know, my lady. Lord Hugh was in possession of insider information... regarding your marriage. It is no secret that some in Britain believe his highness should have made a better choice of bride. I am not one of them," Dora hastened to add.

"Why not?"

"That should be obvious. It would be the greatest hypocrisy for me, of all people, to stand in the way of anyone's life choices. According to Lady Tabitha, Lord Hugh felt the same. When he uncovered details about the plan, he resigned himself to the necessity of warning his lifelong friend. He intended to speak with Bertie the night of the engagement party, but he was killed before he could do so."

Lady Elizabeth's eyes glittered with tears. The timely arrival of a footman bearing tea offered her a moment to recover. While he laid a tablecloth and set out the pot, porcelain cups, and a plate of iced cakes, Elizabeth strode to the window.

Her shoulders shook, but she didn't make a sound. Dora

desperately wanted to offer the woman some comfort, but the presence of the footman stilled her hand. When he finally left, she searched for the energy to rise. Elizabeth turned around before she found it.

Her face was dry, but the pink tinge to her cheeks betrayed her choked back sobs. "Will you forgive me if I admit something terrible? We are strangers, and yet, right now, I have no one else whom I can trust. It is clear Lady Tabitha has taken you into her confidence. And today, you risked yourself to save me. Surely that moves us past acquaintances?"

Dora stilled completely, no longer feeling the pain from her bruises. She kept all hints of guile from her expression. "I am better at keeping a confidence than almost anyone else in the world, my lady. And I'd consider it an honour to be your friend."

Her truthful answer achieved the desired outcome. Lady Elizabeth rushed back and sat beside Dora on the divan. She pulled a handkerchief from her sleeve and dried her eyes while Dora patted her on the arm.

"I'm afraid I'm making a horrendous mistake, Theodora. How many times must I second-guess my decision to marry Bertie? The irony is, I feared losing my autonomy and control. Yet, it is only through my sheer determination not to back down that I am still here."

"You truly love him?"

"I do." Elizabeth chuckled. "I didn't think that was enough. Did you know that? It is why I said no for so long."

"If it isn't too bold of me to ask, what changed your mind? Why do you choose to stay?" Dora was asking as much for her own curiosity as for the investigation. What made someone fly in the face of such a strong and constant headwind?

"Because Bertie and I are better together. It took his mother to convince me of it, but I now know it is the truth. While I pray every day that he be spared the throne, until Edward settles down and has children, it remains a possibility. In such a case, Bertie will need someone in his corner whose loyalty is beyond a shadow of a doubt. Someone to remind him he is capable. That is something I can do."

Dora's life was far removed from that of the royal family, yet she felt an immediate kinship with Lady Elizabeth. Dora's relationship with Rex found strength from being built on a similar foundation. Although she needed no more reasons to see this case through to the end, this gave her fuel to carry on.

"May I speak frankly, Elizabeth?"

"After all I've said so far? Of course. You needn't ask!"

"One needs only to listen to the rumour mill to know why Bertie should not marry you. For now, let's set him aside. I want to know something else. What of you? Is there anyone who might want you to choose someone else?"

"Me? I'm hardly important," Elizabeth scoffed.

"You do yourself a disservice. You must have had other suitors, perhaps even other requests for your hand?"

Elizabeth shook her head. "I was not the debutante of the year. I had no wish to be. The closest I came to making other arrangements was a childhood promise to marry a friend. Given we were twelve at the time, I hardly considered it binding."

Dora agreed, but she asked a follow-up question, nonetheless. "Who was your first beau?"

"It was Rupert. We practically grew up together. After the palace announced our engagement, he was the first to pledge his everlasting friendship. So you see, Theodora, there is no reason to believe he wishes me harm."

Lady Elizabeth truly believed what she said, but Dora wasn't so sure.

Rupert was a snake in the grass. It remained to be seen whether he was a harmless grass snake or a poisonous adder.

Chapter 21
Revisiting the Evidence

Harris cornered Rex the moment he walked in the door. "We need to discuss how we're going to handle Dora."

"Handle her?" Rex stopped Harris there. "I told you when I phoned from the castle. She said she's fine. I kept an eye on her while we walked to the Rolls and during the drive back from Windsor. She's holding up better than I expected."

Harris crossed his arms and refused to budge. "Have you forgotten about the famous British stiff upper lip? Dora's is made of reinforced steel. I'm telling you, she's lying, mate. She could be missing a limb and still claim to be perfectly fit. If we want her to rest today, we'd best strategise a plan."

Rex remained doubtful, but Harris wasn't going to be fobbed off. He decided to buy himself time to speak with Dora. She'd gone in ahead of him, saying she wanted to get changed out of her riding habit. He unbuttoned his coat and handed it to Harris. "Let me put on clean clothes and we can discuss. Meet you in the library in five minutes?"

Rex took the stairs two at a time, equally eager to see how Dora was getting on as to be out of his sweaty clothes. On the first floor, their bedroom sat at the end of the hall. He opened the door to their room, caught sight of Dora's bruised torso, and closed it just as fast.

Harris was waiting for him at the top of the staircase. "Now, do you believe me?"

"Egads, Harris! Her entire right side is purple! How did you know?"

"Inga and I were there when she decided to master bareback riding in the Sahara. She heals fast, but even so, if she doesn't take it easy today, she'll pay for it in the future."

"How on earth are we meant to get her to rest? Tie her to the chair?"

Harris choked back a laugh. "As entertaining as that sight would be, I do have a fondness for my head. As soon as she got free of the ties, she'd come running for us. No, there's only one tactic that works, and that is to give Miss Laurent a taste of her own medicine."

Rex scrunched his brow but couldn't come up with an appropriate answer. "We should pretend to be someone else?"

"I wish," Inga said, coming up the stairs. "What Harris meant is we must somehow convince Dora that having a quiet day in is her idea. Not ours, and certainly not because the doctor said so. All tactics, devious or otherwise, are on the table. Do you understand?"

Rex nodded his head, despite not being sure he'd understood at all.

Inga scowled at him. "Come along. I'll show you how it's done." She strode past Rex and continued until she reached the door to his room. She rapped twice on the wooden surface and then went inside.

Dora had managed to change into her favourite kimono. At first glance, she was the picture of health. But Rex couldn't help but notice that she was favouring her left side.

Inga showed no signs of sympathy. If anything, she

motioned for Dora to move faster. "Finally, you made it back. I was worried all Cook's work would be for naught."

Dora's forehead creased. "What work?"

"Why, the special lunch she offered to prepare. Last night, remember? You remarked on how cold it would be during your morning ride, and she said she'd whip up a warm meal for your return." Inga leaned in and asked in a lowered voice, "You do remember that, right? Rex said you didn't hit your head that hard..."

"Of course. How could I forget such a kind offer?" Dora said, lying through her teeth, just as Inga expected. "What are we having?"

"A full roast dinner. She got a turkey from the butcher, roasted it with potatoes and carrots, and she even made your favourite Yorkshire puddings."

Rex's stomach grumbled while Inga rattled off the rest of the menu. Each course was heavier than the last. By the time they finished dessert, even he would need a nap.

Which, he recognised, was Inga's plan all along. The crafty woman must have leapt into action as soon as Rex telephoned with the news of Dora's incident.

The rest of the afternoon went swimmingly. After a long rest, Rex professed to having a tickle in the back of his throat. Inga ordered cups of hot tea and biscuits for them all. Toward evening, Dora got the itch to start moving. Harris arrived with the morning papers they'd all forgotten to read. Given reading the dailies was Dora's own rule, she could hardly say no.

After dinner was done, Rex allowed himself a sigh of relief. They'd accomplished the impossible — keeping the indomitable Theodora Laurent off her feet for eight straight hours. Now they were ensconced in the sitting room, with the curtains drawn, the fire burning, and no reasons at all for them to leave. Rex handed Dora her current read and then fished his chosen novel from the stack of books in the room. Curled up as they were on the sofa, Rex was looking forward to a quiet night.

Inga and Harris arrived in short order, choosing a pair of armchairs. Harris unbuttoned his coat, revealing his newest, flamboyant cummerbund. Inga rolled her eyes at the sight of the yellow daisies dancing across his waist. Unlike her partner, she had avoided any flamboyant choice of clothing. That evening, she wore a wool dress in simpler shades of maroon and ivory. Rex noted that they set off her chestnut hair nicely.

The final addition to their intimate circle was Rex's cat Mews. The orange tabby leapt onto the armrest beside Rex and began kneading the expensive upholstery. Dora growled at the cat in annoyance, but he ignored her. Their uneasy truce survived only because Rex demanded they make peace.

He'd no sooner opened the book in his hands than Dora got to her feet. She sauntered to the middle of the room and clapped her hands to get everyone's attention.

"Excellent job of making me recuperate, everyone, but it is time to bring the farce to an end. We still have a murder to solve and a princess-to-be to save. We can't afford for me to malinger any longer."

Inga covered her chest with her hand. "Why, Dora! I do not know what you mean."

"You overplayed your hand when Cook served Christmas dinner for lunch. If I didn't love Yorkshire puddings so much, I'd have called you on the carpet sooner. But enough is enough. The attack on Elizabeth has drastically altered our timeline. Given Clark was locked in at Lord Audley's at the time of the shooting, I expect he will soon be eliminated as a suspect. With his release, so, too, goes our excuse for investigating."

"It's worse than that," Rex admitted. "The king and queen will never forgive Audley if something happens to Elizabeth, especially since he's kept them in the dark. We have to solve this mystery within the next twenty-four hours. After that, Audley will be forced to come clean."

Inga raised her hands and motioned for them to remain calm. "We work best under pressure. Rather than agonising over the worst-case scenario, let's revisit what we know so far."

"I'll grab a pen and paper," Harris offered.

"And four glasses of Port, while you're up." Dora grimaced in pain when she returned to her seat. "It will help me feel more comfortable, and I'd prefer not to drink alone."

Once they all had a glass in hand, Dora began offering her thoughts. "The night of the engagement party, Tabitha was due to speak with Prince Bertie, thanks to the arrangements we put in place. Hugh went ahead to make sure all was safe, entering the room while no one was looking."

"Someone must have been watching," Inga countered. "His actions caught the killer's eye. The killer followed Hugh into the Semi-State room. They spoke, and the killer stabbed him."

"Indeed," Dora conceded. "Then I discovered the body and had to leap into action with a new plan. At the time, I didn't know whether Hugh was the sender of Audley's anonymous notes or not. I found that out after I spoke with Tabitha. She also provided us with a list of suspects."

Harris scribbled three names on his notepad. "Our suspects are Bertie's nearest and dearest- Nicholas, Rupert, and Thomas, Tabitha's own brother."

"Tabitha exonerated her brother, which came as little surprise. I didn't, however, take either of them at their word. Rex, did Brantley find out anything through the servant network?"

Rex had asked his valet to investigate whether the twins were truly as dedicated to one another as they claimed. "Brantley plays cards with Thomas's valet. He verified the twins' statements. Said the man whinged on about Thomas holding Tabitha's opinion on his clothing in higher regard than his own."

"Very well, I'll cross him off." Harris drew a line. "What of Nicholas and Rupert?"

"On paper, Nicholas has the stronger motivation. His cousin was on the potential bride list." Dora added, "Nicholas said his cousin is due to announce her own engagement. But what if he fudged the timing? What if she hasn't announced her marriage because she's waiting to see if Bertie's engagement falls apart?"

"So, do I cross his name off or not?" Harris asked. When neither Dora nor Rex answered, he made on his own decision.

"What did you write?" Rex asked.

"A question mark and a note to look further into the cousin. We have only Nicholas's statement that her engagement is pending."

"Excellent point, dear," Inga said, smiling at her partner. "Spoken like a true retired police officer."

"All that's left is Rupert. I spoke with him," Rex said. "He claimed he had no issue with Bertie and Elizabeth having a relationship, but he thought it should be more informal."

Harris looked up from his notes. "Informal? Like an affair? A royal affair?"

"He'd hardly be the first royal to engage in such extracurricular activities," Dora pointed out. "But it would be very out of character."

Rex held up a finger to stop her. "Less than you might think. Rupert offered the story of Bertie's past dalliance as proof."

"I still don't like it," Dora argued. "How did Rupert react to the shooting?"

Rex scrunched his brow. "Weirdly, he was the most upset of all. He said he'd be devastated if anything happened to her."

"And yet, he was fine with the idea of Bertie dragging her into a scandal." Dora took a sip of her wine. "Elizabeth said something to me which might be relevant. She and Rupert had a childhood agreement to wed one day."

"Are we holding people to decisions they made in their youth?" Inga asked. "Most of us grow up and discover what we really want is far different. Case in point, all of us."

Rex conceded Inga had a point. He'd once proposed to a doe-eyed village girl with the most glorious riot of curls and a reputation for being fast. The stable master had discovered them locking lips and had put a stop to their burgeoning relationship.

He eyed Dora and decided to keep that story to himself.

"If there's nothing else, we've got two names with question marks beside them," Harris said, pulling Rex back to the present. "In both cases, we don't have enough information for Lord Audley to take action."

When Harris set down his pen, Inga cleared her throat. "Perhaps it is time we review the night of the engagement in full. I know you all carry guilt for your choices, and would prefer to turn a blind eye on certain parts. However, the time for regret is past. Cast your minds back to the moments after Dora discovered Hugh's body. Was there anything you might have missed?"

Chapter 22
The Missing Moment

BACK AT THE ENGAGEMENT PARTY
Dora wrapped her arms around herself and sank deeper into the shadows of the Eastern Terrace gardens. Although she stood perfectly still, her mind was a whirlwind of activity.

They'd arrived with a simple aim - follow Prince Bertie to the meeting with the anonymous letter writer and uncover their identity.

Instead, she'd found a dead man, the corpse warm and blood still dripping.

She and Rex would have to remain involved. That much was clear. But they also had to protect their identity as agents of the government at all costs.

Threading this needle would be far from easy. If anything, there, in the cold wintry air, Dora felt an icy tendril of fear slide down her back.

She was accustomed to being on her own, putting no one's life at risk but hers. However, here in England, she had Rex, her parents, her brother, and even the Dowager Duchess, to take into account. She vowed to do whatever it took to keep everyone safe - her and Rex, their family and friends, and the royal family.

She leaned over to get a better view of the terrace. Two men were coming her way. Backlit by the flood of lights coming from the ballroom, their faces were hidden. Dora recognised them nonetheless. The muscular man with the easy stride was Rex. The other, however, was not Harris.

The shorter man with the upright carriage and precise step was none other than Lord Audley.

Dora gave silent thanks to Harris's ability to seemingly read her mind. Her big problem was going to require big thinkers. No one was better than the devious spy master himself.

"Over here," she hissed when they got within earshot.

Rex flicked his lighter and pretended to light a cigarette, providing him and Lord Audley with an excuse to be outside. He puffed in the wintry air, letting a cloud of breath fill in for the missing smoke.

It took Dora seconds to tell her partner and her mentor about her grisly discovery. Rex choked back a swear word.

Dora was more interested in what Lord Audley had to say. The man always thought three moves ahead. She waited for him to nod or move or utter something to show he'd foreseen this outcome.

But he didn't. Lord Audley remained completely still, as if her news had struck him dumb.

For the first time in a long while, Dora worried. She'd had plenty of things go wrong in the past, even in high-profile assignments. But Windsor Palace? Involving a prince? And Lord Audley was thrown for a loop?

None of this boded well for their futures.

Before Dora's concerns could spiral any deeper toward despair, Lord Audley got a hold of himself.

He turned to Dora. "It's a foregone conclusion that you two

must investigate. Perhaps you should go back in and stumble across the body."

Dora remembered the pinched faces of the society matrons. They'd call for her head. "I can't find the body. There's too high a risk that I will get the blame, at least at first."

"I can ensure you don't end up in a cell," Audley assured her.

"Thanks, but that isn't my concern. If I'm painted as guilty, even for a moment, that will severely limit my ability to ask questions. Everyone will wonder about my motives."

Lord Audley huffed, his breath puffing into the air.

Think, Dora. Think!

Rex came to her rescue. "What if someone else discovers the body? Someone with a connection to us, even if tenuous. Like when Freddie died. No one thought twice about me getting involved. Or you, for that matter."

"That might work," Dora agreed.

Faces flashed through her mind. Whom had she seen in the ballroom? Harris? Rex's grandmother? Her parents? She raised and discarded options until she landed on one that might work. A sly grin crossed her face.

"We could arrange for Benedict to find the corpse. He always wants to be involved. Father could demand Lord Audley help. And Rex, you two have been known to raise a glass."

Rex shivered. "Benedict won't thank you for dragging his sterling reputation through the mud."

"That's half my fun," Dora admitted with a dark chuckle. "Lord Audley, you can keep him out of jail and out of our investigation. He would not truly be at risk."

"As much as I'd delight in watching you tweak your brother's and your father's noses, your plan has a fatal flaw."

Dora ran through her words, but couldn't find the problem. "What is it?"

"Benedict's sterling reputation. He has no motive. If someone found him standing over a body, they'd assume he was trying to save them." Lord Audley's grim face dared her to contradict his words. "Time is running out. If we're going to find a solution, we need to do so now."

Conjuring a murder suspect from thin air was fast becoming the biggest challenge of Dora's life. She was no stranger to operating under pressure, but never before had so much been at risk. Life had been simpler when she'd worked on her own. A few words in the right ear and she could talk her way out of any trouble.

This time, they needed someone who could talk their way into a murder rap. It was hardly a common skill, even amongst the wildest in their set. She was Goldilocks, facing a line of suspects. Too well-behaved, too old, too far removed. How was she meant to find someone just right?

Rex flinched. He was standing so close to Dora that his movement jostled her.

"What is it?" she asked. "Is someone coming?"

"No..." Rex allowed the word to linger in the air, his voice trailing off.

Dora moved around until she could look him in the face. His eyes shifted, never staying long enough to focus. When he caught her staring, he rubbed the back of his neck.

Dora knew how to interpret his body language.

"You have an idea. Someone here. Someone we can frame."

"I..." Rex avoided her eyes. He jammed his hands in his pockets. "It's a terrible idea. It won't work. Besides, we can't."

"Can't what?" Audley asked. "Given the dire situation, I assure you that we can."

"Whoever it is cannot be any worse than me suggesting my own brother," Dora assured Rex in a soft tone. She patted him on the chest. "No judgement, we promise."

Rex took a fortifying breath. "There's someone here tonight. Someone we know well. Someone with a possible motive."

"Don't hold back on us now," Audley ordered, like a general on the field.

Rex stepped aside and turned his back on Dora and Audley. With his gaze fixed on the flag flying above the castle keep, he shoved down the guilt of his betrayal.

"There's only one person here who fits the bill. He told me earlier he owes Lord Hugh money. He lost at cards, but was so inebriated he forgot to make good on the debt. I was standing beside him when he saw Lord Hugh across the room and the memory jogged loose."

Dora's stomach tightened. She desperately hoped she was wrong, even though all her instincts screamed she was correct.

"Clark?"

Rex gave a single nod. His shoulder tightened in preparation for the blow of disapproval.

Dora couldn't let him bear the guilt alone. He'd done enough. She'd take it from there.

"Lord Clark Kenworthy. Everyone knows we're friends. We'd be expected to rush to his aid. As much as I hate saying this, he's the perfect solution." *And also, their only solution.*

Lord Audley was never one to allow sentiment to rule his decisions. "Does Lord Clark have money problems?"

"No. That's what makes him ideal. After the rush to blame, his motive will crumble under scrutiny. Society will deem him innocent soon enough, even if the police take longer to clear his name."

Lord Audley's eyes brightened. "His reputation has more dents in it than my first car. Another knock or two is only likely to enhance it."

"We will have to make it up to him," Dora said. "Even if he

doesn't know we're responsible, we will. I don't want that on my conscience." *Or Rex's.*

Audley patted Rex on the arm, drawing him into the conversation. He made him a promise. "If push comes to shove, I'll do everything in my power to guarantee he doesn't suffer any ill consequences.'" Lord Audley gritted his teeth and then added, "Including going to the king with the full story."

Dora launched into motion. There was no time for second thoughts. They had to move.

"Then it's settled. We send Clark a note, telling him to go to the Crimson room. Harris can take care of it."

Audley agreed. "Have him sign the note from Rex. That will give you two an additional reason to work on clearing his name."

Rex ran his hands over his hair, the decision resting heavy on his conscience. If Dora had to guess, it felt like an elephant crushing his chest.

She knew that pressure well. Like it or not, it was a milestone in his newfound career.

She tugged his chin her way and gave him a smile. "Welcome to the difficult life of being a spy."

Rex scowled at Dora, clearly not appreciating her troubling reassurances.

"Get a move on," Audley commanded them, already backing away. "You know the appointed time. Be on the dance floor by then."

"Good point. I've been gone for a while as it is. Rex, you find Harris. I'll let one of the men on my dance card have a spin. You can cut in when all is in place."

With that, the trio went their separate ways. Lord Audley left first, retracing his steps to the ballroom. Rex headed to where he had left Harris.

Dora took a side path to the far ballroom door. She spotted one of her eager suitors standing nearby and approached.

While he twirled her around, she took note of where everyone was standing.

Prince Bertie's closest friends were all present and accounted for. All except Lord Hugh, that was. Dora noted their expressions and positions. Two stood watching Prince Bertie. One man, however, only had eyes for Lady Elizabeth.

Chapter 23
Undercover, At Last

BACK IN DORA'S SITTING ROOM Inga shook her head and frowned at the pair. "I still cannot believe you set Clark up to take the fall."

"Only temporarily," Rex said in a rush. "And as promised, Lord Audley ensured he has yet to spend a night behind bars."

"But a murder rap?" Inga was still stunned. She pointed at Dora. "You've pulled many tricks in your life, but this one takes the cake."

Rex held up a hand to forestall Inga from making further comment. "You can flagellate us later. Right now, I'm more interested in what Dora said at the end of her recollection. Who was fixated on Elizabeth?"

"It didn't seem significant at the time, but now..."

"Well, don't leave us in suspense." Inga waved Dora on.

"It was Rupert. He was standing on the opposite side of the room from the royal couple. I couldn't miss the naked longing in his eyes. I assumed he was watching some woman spin around the floor. But now that I think on it again, it's equally possible he was staring at Elizabeth. She was across from him, chatting with a group of women."

Harris reopened his notepad. "Let's assume you are correct. Rupert is in love with Lady Elizabeth and will do anything to keep her from marrying Bertie. What are you going to do with this information? It is hardly enough to prove his guilt."

"He's right," Rex agreed. "How would we explain this to Prince Bertie? The only proof we have is that he and Elizabeth enjoyed a childhood crush. It's a long way from there to stabbing someone. If we want Bertie to believe us, we need a smoking gun, proverbial or otherwise."

Dora stood up, moving faster than Rex expected. "We won't find anything here. We have to search his home."

Rex latched onto Dora's wrist, stopping her from dashing off. "For what? Bloodied gloves? A rifle and a scope? He was with us yesterday. He couldn't have taken the shot at Elizabeth."

Rex might as well have held his tongue. After an afternoon of inaction, Dora was champing at the bit to do something, to do anything to bring this mystery to an end. She twisted her hand around until she was holding onto him.

She tugged on Rex's arm, urging him to hurry. "He must have hired someone. Maybe we'll find their communications. The bottom line is this is our last lead."

Mews howled his protest at Rex's departure. Rex felt the same as his cat. Dora was bruised and battered. The last thing she needed to do was go traipsing about town.

Rex resisted her pull. "We can go tomorrow, or I can get the twins to accompany me."

"I'm going now, with or without you," Dora said, holding his gaze. Determination was stamped into the twinkle in her eyes and jut of her jaw. "I've been sitting around all afternoon, twiddling my thumbs."

"Because you fell off a horse," Inga reminded her.

Dora glanced at her over her shoulder. "As you well know, I've been hurt worse and still upheld my duties."

"That is far less reassuring than you might think," Rex countered. Her tight grasp on his arm didn't loosen.

"Think about it, Rex. Now is the perfect time for us to go. Rupert is likely out for the night. We can sneak in, check his private chambers, and then we'll go. Twenty minutes, max."

Rex looked at Harris and Inga for their opinions. They wore equally pained expressions, but neither offered a counter-argument.

Rex handled his loss with aplomb. "Fine, but at the first hint of trouble, or first sign of suffering, we're leaving."

"It won't come to that," Dora assured him. She turned as Rex rose to his feet. "Change into dark clothes and don't you dare dawdle."

Harris had the car running by the time they came outside. They piled into the back of Dora's black Model-T, a car so ubiquitous on London's streets as to be invisible. It was the ideal choice for late-night sleuthing.

Rupert lived alone in a spacious townhouse a stone's throw from Buckingham Palace. He might not have the title and pedigree of his neighbours, but few of them could count a royal prince amongst their closest companions.

Harris dropped Dora and Rex off a short distance from the house. They took advantage of the private garden across the street to get the lay of the land.

The three-story home stood on the corner of two quiet streets. The pair had no trouble guessing at the layout. The wide windows on the ground floor would be the public rooms. Narrower windows above allowed light into the family bedrooms. The top floor with its dormer windows was the servants' domain.

Although there was no sign from the front, both were sure there was a lower floor hidden from view where the kitchen and other workrooms were located.

Rex and Dora both had been in dozens of homes like this one. That was to their advantage. They had a much better chance of getting in and out without being caught if they knew their way around.

Rex turned to Dora. She, too, was making a careful study of the Georgian townhouse. In her tailored black trousers and thick wool sweater, with her flat cap pulled low, she appeared to the rest of the world as a young man on the cusp of adulthood.

Rex, however, knew the shape of her hidden curves by heart. He marvelled at her ability to maintain her stiff upper lip against the soreness of her limbs. The sooner they put this wild hare idea of hers to bed, the better.

"What do you make of it?" he whispered to get her attention.

"Much as I expected. The curtains are tight on the ground floor, but if the lights were on, we'd see a glow around the edges." She pointed toward the roofline. "Lights are on upstairs. Likely the housemaids and footman are turning in for the night. With Rupert out, they can take advantage of an early bedtime."

Rex found no fault with her logic. "How do you want to go in? First floor bedrooms?"

"If we can find a way to get up there. Let's circle around to get a view of the rear."

Rex and Dora almost always preferred to enter through a dark bedroom window. They were least likely to cross paths with a servant there. However, that plan had a fatal flaw that became clear as they peered over the garden fence.

"Stuff and bother! I can't see any way to get up there," Dora grumbled. Indeed, there were no balconies, trellises, nor even a sturdy tree branch.

"Okay, ground floor it is. Good thing I brought my lock picks." Rex pulled the small set of tools from his pocket. The garden gate unlocked with ease. Deep shadows allowed them to approach quickly.

Off to the side was a narrow concrete staircase leading down to the servant's entrance to the kitchens. They steered away from it, ducking low as they moved behind a line of shrubs. Two sets of elaborately carved French doors led into the house. Which one to choose?

The dining room was likely to be above the kitchen. Rex rationalised that the other doors likely led to a study or sitting room. He pointed toward them and Dora nodded her agreement.

After picking the door lock, Rex nudged the curtain aside. Faint moonlight showed thick carpets, a cold fireplace, and the gilt edge of a picture frame. They crept in, closing the door behind themselves, and tugged the curtain shut again.

Dora stole across the room on silent feet and listened at the doorway. She heard no sound. Confident they were alone and unnoticed, she flicked on the torch she'd brought in. The narrow beam of light revealed the room to be a study.

"Check the bookshelves while I go through the desk, "she ordered in a hushed whisper. They searched methodically, but faster than most would expect. They were, after all, trained professionals. Unlike thieves, they'd mastered the art of getting in and out of homes and offices without leaving a trace.

"Nothing here so far," Rex murmured.

"I've had no luck either," Dora muttered. "Let's move upstairs."

Rex motioned for Dora to check the hallway while he put the books he'd pulled out back into place. Most of the thick leather bindings had unbroken spines.

Although they hadn't found a smoking gun, or a smoking anything, Rex's opinion of Rupert had dropped. What was the point of owning a book you never opened? Rex could imagine Dora's thoughts on the matter.

"The hallway is clear," Dora said, motioning for him to hurry. Rex slid the last book into place and moved away from the shelf. He circled around the back of an overstuffed armchair to avoid bumping into a curio cabinet. It would be a nasty twist of fate for them to make it this far only to have him send a display of figurines crashing to the ground.

A floorboard creaked.

"What was that?" Dora whispered. She checked the hallway. "It didn't come from out there."

Rex had frozen in place at her words. When she raised an eyebrow in a silent question, he shifted his weight. The floor squeaked again.

Dora's eyes lit up. She closed the door firmly and twisted the lock before coming his way. Rex had already dropped to his knees. He shoved aside the rug to reach the wooden floor underneath.

Dora shined her light across the plank until they spotted a narrow, finger-sized indentation in one end. Dora motioned for Rex to get on with it. He held his breath as he carefully lifted the end. It came free with only a soft scrape.

Below the floor was a shallow space the size and shape of the floorboard. Rex spotted a leather-bound notebook in addition to folded, faded newsprint, letters, and photos.

Dora's need to know spurred her into action. She gathered the top most materials and flipped through them while Rex watched.

There was a common theme. The same name and face appeared again and again.

Rex took out the notebook. Unlike the books on the shelves, this one was much used. The pages were dog-eared and filled with a near-illegible scribble. One name, however, was clear — Elizabeth.

"Should we wait for Rupert and confront him with our findings?"

Dora thought for a moment before answering. "No, we need a neutral ground for this confrontation. Grab everything and stuff it into your coat. We're getting out of here."

"Where are we taking this? Home?"

"For now. But tomorrow, we're taking all this to Lord Audley."

They were so close to achieving their objectives. The documents in Rex's pocket would definitely clear Clark's name. Hugh's killer would be unmasked. Prince Bertie and Lady Elizabeth would be safe.

But for how long?

Once they were safely home, Rex's stomach lurched at the thought of Clark's last few days. He'd been a pawn of last resort in a deadly game. Yes, Lord Audley had ensured his safety, but that barely lessened the guilt Rex and Dora shared. Rex couldn't tell him everything. That would place Clark in an even worse situation. His safety lay in his lack of awareness. He must never know that his closest friends were spies.

But Rex couldn't say the same about Prince Bertie. If Audley had his way, he'd hush up the whole affair. It was what he did for the good of the nation.

What about the good of the man and woman? Was Bertie really better off not knowing about the treachery of the rest of his friends?

The questions swirled in Rex's mind while he dressed for bed. This was no hypothetical situation. If he got this wrong, the repercussions would be serious — for him, Dora, and Prince Bertie. Indecision kept Rex awake long after Dora succumbed to her exhaustion.

Rex waited until Dora awoke the next morning, moving with much greater ease, to ask for her opinion on the matter. What did she believe they should do?

Her brow wrinkled in contemplation. Like him, she recognised it was far from a simple question. However, she arrived at a conclusion much more quickly.

"I must admit, my inclinations are usually in line with Lord Audley's. However, you have raised a fair point. Perhaps it is time we started focusing less on the throne and more on the man who might one day sit upon it."

Chapter 24
The Big Reveal

T he first person they rang was Clark. After the attempt on
Elizabeth's life, DCI Miller had agreed to allow Clark to
return home. As always, he was thrilled to hear from them. His
sentiments soared to new heights when they shared their news.
They had identified the real killer. Better yet, they wanted his
help with the grand unveiling.

They were to meet Lord Audley at his home promptly at
two in the afternoon. Although he expected them to come alone,
they had other plans. At the appointed time, Rex rapped on the
heavy brass door knocker. Lord Audley's butler answered the
door.

If the butler was surprised to find three people standing
there instead of the expected two, he gave no hint. He did,
however, adopt a brisk pace ahead of Lord Audley's guests to
make sure he'd be able to announce them.

"Three visitors for you, Your Grace."

"Three?"

Dora bit back a smile at the confusion in Audley's voice.

"Yes. It appears that Lord Rex and Miss Laurent collected
Lord Clark along their way." The butter moved aside to allow

said guests to enter the drawing room where Lord Audley was sitting.

"Back so soon, Lord Clark?" Audley asked after welcoming them inside.

"Only for a brief visit this time," Clark assured him. "Rex insisted I accompany him."

"I thought it was only right that Lord Clark should be the one to unveil Hugh's killer." Rex wiggled his eyebrows at Lord Audley.

"Of course, absolutely," Audley agreed. "Miss Laurent, shall I ring for tea?"

"Yes, Your Grace, and also more chairs, if you don't mind. We expect the others to arrive shortly."

"How many people have you invited to my home, might I ask?" Audley kept his tone light, but the firm set to his mouth told Dora more than any words.

He was unhappy, and rightfully so. The night before, when they'd returned home, Dora had rung to apprise Lord Audley that their investigation was at an end. He'd given them a time to visit with a full explanation.

However, after Rex's near sleepless night of deep thoughts, Dora had agreed to a different approach. She didn't dare ring the spymaster to ask permission. She'd told Rex she worried Audley would not agree. In truth, she preferred to ask for forgiveness, rather than plead for approval.

Dora trusted that by the end of the afternoon, Lord Audley would understand why she and Rex had acted as they did.

For now, the older man was staring at her, waiting for an answer to his question about how many chairs they needed.

"We'll be ten in total, Your Grace."

To Audley's credit, he did as she asked, and even let her take charge in directing the footman on the placement of the extra seating.

While the men made small talk, Dora staged the room into an unusual tableau. If one studied it closely, they'd see it was more like a courtroom than an upper-class social.

As the remainder of the invited guests arrived, Dora directed them to their places. First up were Prince Bertie and Lady Elizabeth. Dora motioned them toward a silk-covered chaise big enough for two. Nicholas and Rupert were next. As the prime suspects, Dora sat them in two of the three wooden chairs near the fire. Clark took the third.

The last two guests to arrive were the twins, Thomas and Tabitha. Dora had a sofa ready for them. Tabitha took care to sit in the middle, leaving an empty place beside her for Dora to join them.

Dora stopped short of telling Audley where to sit. He sized up the situation and chose to remain standing by the fire, looking very much at ease as he rested an elbow on the mantle.

Although they were in Lord Audley's home, Prince Bertie was the highest ranking individual. "We're all here, but I daresay I don't know why. Could someone explain? Lord Audley?"

Audley waved Rex forward.

Rex took centre stage. He and Dora agreed that he should be the one to talk. As far as everyone knew, he was the one Lord Audley tasked with being involved. Clark was also his best friend. It was best for Dora if everyone believed her to be nothing more than Rex's current choice of companion.

Rex cleared his throat and surveyed the room. The royal couple sat across from him, ready to play the part of the judge, even if they didn't yet know it.

The line of suspects was on his left, and Dora and the twins were on his right. Dora had weighed the idea of sitting Thomas with the other men, but just as quickly discarded it. She'd long since dismissed him as a suspect, and Tabitha needed all the support she could get.

Even now, Thomas had Tabitha's right hand enveloped in his. Dora reached over and took her left.

Rex waited until Dora gave a nod of approval for him to begin.

"I am sure you can all guess why we are here. Lord Hugh is dead. Lady Elizabeth is under threat. Lord Clark stood accused of a terrible crime. Some might say these are reasons enough to postpone your wedding."

Prince Bertie's neck flushed with anger at the mere suggestion.

Rex didn't let that slow him down. "Some of those people are here in this room. I am not one of them," he hastened to add.

Dora kept her attention fixed on the royals. Prince Bertie's ire was not abating. Lady Elizabeth, however, remained more circumspect. There was no hint of shock or surprise.

Elizabeth knew. Perhaps she sensed the hidden animosity of Bertie's friends. Or maybe someone had dropped enough hints. Either way, she kept quiet, more interested in letting this play out than in revealing her hand.

Rex continued, "There are rare instances when a man is justified in keeping secrets. For example, in times of war, when speaking would threaten peace. Equally, there comes a moment when speaking up is required."

Rex directed his attention to Prince Bertie. "You made the brave choice to marry for love, despite your so-called royal duties. Your friends here- Lord Thomas, Lord Nicholas, and Rupert felt you chose wrong. They took it upon themselves to intervene at all costs."

Prince Bertie tore his gaze from Rex and looked at his friends. "Is this true?"

Nicholas and Rupert stared at the floor, too embarrassed to meet his eyes. Only Thomas owned up to his part.

"I was an utter and complete fool, Bertie. I will spend the rest of my days regretting my choice."

"He will, indeed," Rex agreed. "Of all your friends, Lord Hugh was the only man brave enough to stand up to the others. When they ignored him, Lady Tabitha chose to take action. She sent the anonymous note to Lord Audley, asking him to arrange for a private conversation."

"I thought you'd be more inclined to listen if Lord Audley added his gravitas," Tabitha explained. "Hugh was furious when I told him what I'd done. He went ahead of me, wanting to smooth everyone's feathers. You know what happened to him."

Rex didn't give them time to react to Tabitha's confession. "Lord Clark was an innocent bystander, and my friend of many years. To aid his cause, I took it upon myself to look into the matter, with Theodora's help. It took some time, but last night, we found the final piece of evidence we needed to identify Hugh's killer. Given he nearly took the blame, I felt it only fair he be the one to share our findings."

Rex motioned for Clark to take the floor. All eyes in the room followed his every move.

"Although Lord Audley was a perfect host, nonetheless I found myself with ample time to question why this happened. Yes, I owed Lord Hugh an unpaid debt. But who kills over an amount they can easily afford? I felt the same when Rex told me how these men plotted to ruin your engagement. I love a clever prank as much as the next, but this was far worse. What kind of friends place duty to the state above the responsibilities of friendship?"

Dora barely avoided flinching. Rex had his jaw clenched so tight, she feared his teeth might break. She reminded herself again that they were not the same as their suspects.

But a tiny voice in the back of her head pointed out that the line of separation was faint.

Like Thomas had promised Bertie, they would make it up to Clark, even if it took them forever.

Clark carried on, entirely comfortable being the centre of attention. "Lady Elizabeth, as much as I regret the danger to your life, the attempted shooting opened our eyes to a new possibility. Miss Laurent was the one to put the puzzle pieces together."

Prince Bertie was mystified. "What do you mean? Someone wanted to hurt Elizabeth because I convinced her to marry me?"

Clark pointed a finger at the men seated on the wooden chairs. "One of those men prioritised duty above all. Had Lady Elizabeth been the granddaughter of a king, he'd have cheered your choice. The other, however, resented not you, but your wife-to-be. He believed that she was the one who'd made the poor choice. In his mind, she was already pledged to him. First, he tried to force you to retract your request for her hand. When that failed, he decided he'd rather escort her to her grave than see her marry someone else."

"Rupert! "Elizabeth gasped, her face the colour of parchment paper. "We were children!"

Bertie opened his mouth to add his fury to the fire. His emotions proved to be too strong for his control over his stutter. His face turned beet red as he stammered, unable to find his words.

"You see!" Rupert exclaimed, jumping to his feet. "Is that who you truly wish to wed? What if he passes his affliction on to your children? You'll curse them, royal blood or not."

"I'd rather gift them with his quiet strength and compassion than worry that they'd inherit your obvious insanity!" Elizabeth hissed in reply. Her back was ramrod straight, and she refused to stand down. She laid a hand upon Bertie's shoulder, lending him her fortitude.

Rupert's eyes flicked around the room as the magnitude of the situation set in. At that moment, everyone there hated him.

"You have no proof I killed Hugh. And I was with you on the ride. How could I have taken the shot?"

"By paying your groomsman to do it for you," Clark said. He pulled a black notebook from his coat pocket. It was the one Dora and Rex found hidden under the floorboard. "You wrote it all here in your private diary. It reads like the rantings of a madman. I'm certain DCI Miller will be most interested in bringing this to the attention of the court of law."

Rupert roared in anger and made a break for the exit. He dashed past the stunned audience and threw open the drawing-room door.

DCI Miller was waiting on the other side, flanked by two hulking policemen. They grabbed his arms and hustled him out the front door to the car waiting at the kerb.

"I beg your pardon for the intrusion, your highnesses," DCI Miller said, doffing his trilby at Prince Bertie and Lady Elizabeth. "If you have no further need of me, I should be on my way."

"Wait," Clark called. He hurried over to hand the detective Rupert's diary.

"Do I want to know how you came to hold this?" the detective asked.

Clark turned to Rex. Rex shook his head. "Best not to look the proverbial gift horse in the mouth." He punctuated his remark with an exaggerated wink.

"I'll go with an anonymous source," DCI Miller agreed.

Clark closed the drawing-room door after the police left.

Bertie was still livid. Thomas and Nicholas were stunned.

Tabitha took a shuttering breath and allowed a sob to escape her lips. She squeezed Dora's hand while Thomas fumbled for his handkerchief. "Thank you for believing me, and for finding justice for Hugh."

"There is no need to say anything," Dora said, taking care to speak with her Theodora Laurent accent. "It kept us from getting into other trouble for a few days."

"It didn't keep you from coming to harm," Lady Elizabeth corrected her. "You are very brave, Miss Laurent. All three of you," she added, including Rex and Clark in her remarks.

Lord Audley intervened before the prince and future princess said anything else. "The important thing is they stopped Rupert before he did anything worse."

"We all owe you a debt. We were blind to his actions," Nicholas confessed. He looked at Bertie. "I won't ask you to forgive me for my part, as what I did was beyond the pale."

"Same for me," Thomas added, glancing between the royals and his sister. "No matter what happens with our friendship, I promise we will support your marriage one hundred per cent."

Dora watched Bertie for his response. He had calmed since Rupert's departure. His shoulders hung as if a new weight had been added to his own back.

"As angry as I am, I also know how easy it is to be led astray by someone who doesn't have your best interest at heart. It will take me time to forget, but I hope to forgive you both much sooner. I have no need for a chorus of yes men, but I do require absolute honesty and forthright conversations. If in doubt, I ask you to think of Hugh. No difference of opinion is worth the cost of your lives."

The group broke up soon after, with everyone going their separate ways. Dora promised to pay a call on Tabitha, this time as a true friend. Dora wouldn't have been surprised if Lady Elizabeth joined them.

Right now, she and Rex had one priority, and one alone. She latched her arm around Clark and guided him out the door.

"Come along, darling. The day is young, our spirits are on the rise, and we're all in need of a dance floor and a strong drink."

"But where will we go?" he asked, glancing back at Rex. "It's three in the afternoon."

Rex pulled a metal object from his pocket. "To Club 43. Its bar is open at any hour if you're lucky enough to have the key."

Chapter 25
The Final Report

Cars lined the Strand near the entrance to The Savoy. Rex hardly took notice anymore of the latest Rolls-Royce, but a bright red Hispano-Suiza caught his eye. Unfortunately, their schedule didn't allow time for a stop, at least not at the Savoy's front door.

Rex and Dora wouldn't be experiencing the luxury of the hotel lobby with crystal chandeliers and a doorman. No bellboy would offer to deliver their luggage, not that they had any with them.

Their stay in the hotel was to be short — very short. In fact, if all went to plan, hardly anyone would know they were there.

"Drop us around back," Dora ordered from her seat beside Rex. Harris, who was driving Dora's new Mercedes-Benz, was happy to oblige. He waited for a gap in the pedestrians before turning into a narrow alley. Another corner brought him to a much less grand exterior.

Harris idled the engine while Rex and Dora surveyed their surroundings. The narrow lane ran between two classic London stone facades. Unlike the Strand, there were no passersby gaping at the grand hotel. Only staff and deliveries used these bland concrete steps.

And, in this case, a pair of undercover spies.

Rex exited first and then turned to offer Dora a hand. Despite their choice of entrance, they were dressed to the nines. Rex used the brim of his hat to shadow his face. Dora hid hers behind a black veil. They stole down the steps and through the door.

A guard waited. He eyed Rex and Dora. They were enough off the beaten path that he should have turned them away. However, their posh frocks stayed his hand.

"We've got a reservation, but the front entrance is rather inhospitable, if you get my drift." Rex slipped the guard a handful of coins. "Photographers and reporters from the gossip rags are parked out front."

The guard grunted his understanding and waved them on. Rex was hardly the first man to sneak a woman other than his wife into the hotel. That was the beauty of the trick.

The whitewashed walls and thin, cheap carpet of the staff area made for a stark comparison to the front of house. Rex and Dora didn't waste any time. He slung his arm over her shoulders and pulled her close. She giggled, playing her role of starry-eyed lovebird to the hilt. The few maids they passed pretended not to see them.

Finally, they came to the stairwell. Rex opened the door. "Ladies first."

Dora arched an eyebrow as she slid past. "Darling, I gave up that title years ago. I think you're concerned I can't make it up in this dress and these heels."

Rex shook his head and motioned her on. "If there is one thing I've learned, it is to never underestimate you."

Dora lifted her long skirt and dashed up two flights of stairs without getting out of breath. On the second floor, they switched to the lift. Rex gave the operator their floor number, and they rode to the top in silence.

Rex found the door marked as the Grand Suite and knocked a familiar rhythm. A faint voice called for them to come in.

Blue and gold carpets blunted the harsh echo of the marble entryway. Lord Audley sat in a chair near the fire, smoking a cigar while he waited for their arrival. He was completely at home, despite the impersonal nature of the setting. With his coat off and his legs crossed, he had the look of a man who had been there for a while.

Who else was he due to meet? His mistress? Another spy?

Rex didn't bother voicing the question. He would not get an answer.

"Did you pass anyone on your way up?" Audley asked after they sat across from him on a velvet sofa.

"One guard, a few maids, and the lift operator. None of them spared us a second glance," Dora assured him.

"Excellent. I won't keep you long since you're clearly on your way elsewhere." Audley puffed on his cigar. "I have an update on Rupert. After that, we should also discuss your next assignment."

Rex braced himself for both topics. They'd neither heard nor read a word about Rupert since the police led him away. Rex feared he'd somehow escaped justice, even though Dora promised him that wasn't possible.

"Rupert agreed to plead guilty in exchange for avoiding a hanging."

Rex released the breath he'd been holding. "That is a relief."

"Indeed. It took some convincing, but we were all keen to avoid any mention of this leaking to the press. In the end, Rupert's parents convinced him to take the deal."

"Surely he didn't expect to be found not guilty!" Dora exclaimed.

"No. The sticking point was a different matter. He didn't want to live knowing Elizabeth was marrying another man."

Rex didn't think he'd ever have sympathy for someone like Rupert. He'd done terrible things, with no regard for those around him.

But if Dora left him for another man... Rex could not even bear the thought.

He slid his hand over an inch until their little fingers touched. Dora somehow understood what he needed because she shifted her hand and intertwined their fingers.

"I'm relieved this is all said and done, especially for Prince Bertie and Lady Elizabeth. They deserve to start their lives together on a happy note," Dora said.

"I agree. That brings us to the two of you. Do you have any preference about what you do next?"

Rex and Dora had batted around ideas one night while snuggling under the covers. He let her take the lead.

"If it is all the same to you, we'd like to go abroad."

"I see... may I ask why?"

"For several reasons," Dora said. "First, I have my family's safety to consider. We've been lucky no one has commented on the similarities in mine and my mother's appearances. It would be wise to put some distance between us. Second, I owe Cynthia and the twins a trip abroad. They've all three made clear their interest in seeing more of the world."

"You said several reasons, but you've only listed two. Was there something else?"

Rex answered Lord Audley. "The last reason is mine. My introduction to this life has hardly been normal, if such a thing can be said to exist. I'd like a chance to explore the other aspects of life as a British spy. To do that, I need to go where fewer people know me."

Lord Audley sat back in his seat and puffed on his cigar. He blew smoke in the air, leaving Rex to worry he'd say no to their request. Rex's palms grew clammy. Dora squeezed his hand.

"How would you feel about Italy?" Audley asked after a pregnant pause. "Mussolini is making movements that have me concerned. We'd benefit from a keener understanding of sentiment on the ground. Assuming you bring your household, you'd be able to speak with people at all levels of society."

Rex glanced at Dora. She gave a single nod. "That works for us. I should warn you, my Italian is shocking."

"Don't worry, dear. I'm fluent, as is Inga." Dora sat up straighter. "Do you need us in Rome right away?"

"No faster than any of your other moves. I assume you'll need time to organise your affairs. And then there is the matter of the royal wedding. I expect invitations will come through for you two."

Dora pulled her hand free from Rex's and lifted it to stop Lord Audley. "Having Theodora Laurent at the wedding will cause too many questions. Same with packing up our home. Lord Reginald Bankes-Fernsby can't abandon England's shores entirely."

Rex's heart skipped a beat. What did Dora mean by that remark? She hadn't raised any concerns before. She'd certainly given no hints she was considering ending their relationship, but would she? Rex hated the doubt that clawed at his insides.

"What are you saying? Are you going without me?"

"Of course not! I'm thinking the exact opposite. Lord Reginald can't move away. Theodora isn't known for staying put. Our public personas are going to have to meet in the middle." Dora took his hands in hers. "We'll travel, darling. An extended trip around the continent. We can ski in the Alps and then work our way south to warm up in Rome."

"And in that time, Rex can polish his Italian," Lord Audley added. "It's a fine plan, Dora. I approve."

"Then it's settled. It will take us a week or two to make all the arrangements and close up my house. Rex and I will update our families, so they won't worry... well, no more so than usual." Dora's comment made both men chuckle.

"Tell them you'll be back in time for the start of the season," Audley suggested. "Otherwise, they may come traipsing after you."

"Perish the thought!" Rex shuddered at the image of his formidable grandmother standing on the prow of an ocean liner, intent on not being left behind. If he didn't give her a definite return date, he wouldn't put it past her.

The mantle clock chimed the hour. Lord Audley tossed the end of his cigar into the fire and rose from his chair. "If there is nothing else, I will let you be on your way."

Their dismissal was so clear that Rex caught himself raising his hand in a salute. He was no longer in the military, but unpicking years of respect to the organisation's hierarchy was another matter.

Rex turned to go, but Dora didn't budge. Before either man could speak, she crossed the room and kissed Lord Audley's cheek.

"What was that for?" the esteemed spy master asked in a stunned voice.

"For many things," Dora replied. She ticked reasons off her fingers. "For not judging us when we framed Clark, for protecting him from suffering, and most of all, for always believing in the two of us."

Only a faint blush revealed how much Lord Audley treasured Dora's words.

He cleared his throat. "Yes, well, your efficiency and success rate speak for themselves. Although, in the future, I'd prefer if you gave me a little warning before inviting members of the royal family into my home. Other than that, keep up the good work."

Rex waited until they were back in the hallway before saying anything. He spun around and stopped Dora in her tracks. "You are incorrigible, you know."

"I do try," she replied. "I know how much you love that about me."

"I love everything about you, Miss Laurent. The good, the bad, and even the downright terrible." Rex lowered his head and kissed her soft lips, marking his claim on her.

When she came up for air, she tweaked his nose. "Let's hope dear Clark feels the same. I've made a slight change to our plans for the evening."

Chapter 26
A Royal Request

C lark glanced out the window with a frown marring his usually amiable countenance. "This isn't the way to the Royal Opera House."

In truth, his quick smile and fast wit had been absent since the day he'd been accused of killing Lord Hugh. Even clearing his name had failed to lift the weight from his shoulders.

He'd made a valiant effort to rejoin society after he and the others unveiled Hugh's killer. By four in the morning, deep in his cups, he admitted that his old life had lost its appeal.

"It is time for me to curb my excesses," he'd declared. "If I hadn't got so sauced that I forgot my own name and my debt to Lord Hugh, I'd never have ended up in that mess."

Clark was partially correct on that point, but that hadn't made his decision to abandon his well-known joie de vivre any easier for everyone to digest.

Only Rex and Dora stuck by his side. They followed his suggestions for three weeks, attending society balls instead of nightclubs and listening to the symphony instead of jazz. But as soon as they recognised that he was as miserable as they were, they'd decided it was time for an intervention.

Normally, such actions were used to convince someone to go straight. This time, they would stop at nothing to remind Clark how much he loved to cut loose and live fancy free.

After all, Dora knew better than anyone the misery of being put in a box. It was no less painful when you were the one making the restrictions.

They hatched a plan. Rex had phoned Clark, claiming to have the usage of his grandmother's box during the opening night performance of Verdi's Rigoletto.

Had Clark given the invitation a second of thought, he'd have realised it was little more than a cover. The Dowager Duchess never failed to attend opening night. But he'd been so grateful for any excuse to leave home that he'd taken the bait.

Now, trapped in the backseat of Dora's Mercedes-Benz, he was powerless to stop their well-intentioned kidnapping.

Dora patted Clark's arm. "That's because we aren't going to the opera. My feet are itching to move in time to the music. We're going to kick up our heels, and I won't take no for an answer."

"But I can't," Clark babbled. He leaned past Dora to look at Rex, who was sitting on the other side of the car. "I'll end up in trouble. You two always get stuck cleaning up my messes. It isn't right."

"It isn't right for you to deny yourself joy, Clark. Enough of living like a monk. If your countenance gets any more dour, even the debutantes will start avoiding you," Rex replied.

"But, but," he stuttered. His mouth said one thing, but his hopeful expression declared another.

Dora knew they had him hooked. Now to reel the line in. "Darling, we are going to take this slowly. No nightclubs. No endless gambling. We may not even see anyone we know. But we are going to dance to the wails of the trumpet and drink while enjoying the dulcet tones of one of my favourite jazz singers." Dora flashed Clark a toothy smile. "You will love it, I promise."

Clark kept up his worried mutterings all the way to their destination. Only the sight of the red brick building with its dignified entrance mollified him enough to get out of the car.

"We've dinner reservations for three, and then a few other friends will join us in the ballroom for dancing. All above board. Nothing scandalous. Will you stay?" Dora asked.

Clark stepped out of the car and stared up at the building. The stalwart hotel with its Mayfair location made it popular with the upper class. It boasted live music and fine cocktails, but also fell in line with the government's liquor laws. It was the perfect choice for a quieter night out — quieter for Clark, anyway.

Clark took a deep breath and slowly exhaled, his shoulders loosening.

Dora claimed her place at his side, slipped her arm through his. "Come along, Clark. As Alexandre Dumas said, '*Never fear quarrels, but seek hazardous adventures.*' Who are we to argue?"

Rex flanked Clark's right and patted his friend on the shoulder. "Dumas also said, '*All for one, and one for all.*' For tonight and so long as you'll claim us as friends, we're in this together."

Clark was momentarily stunned by their show of camaraderie, but he shook it off fast enough. "All for one, indeed. But if it's all the same to you, I insist we each get our own drink."

"I couldn't agree more," Dora purred. She pulled Clark into motion and he followed willingly. All eyes followed the three as they strode through the lobby with nary a care in the world.

During dinner, Dora noted with pleasure that the sparkle was returning to Clark's eyes. Course by course, he unwound until he was once again cracking jokes and having a laugh.

When he excused himself after dessert, Dora made up her mind. She tilted her head toward Rex and whispered under her breath. "We should invite Clark to come on holiday with us."

Rex reared back, his eyebrows knitted. "Is that wise?"

"No," she admitted. "But can you honestly say that abandoning him now is a better choice?"

Rex grimaced and then shook his head. "Let me be the one to ask."

Clark returned, but he wasn't alone. Walking beside him was none other than Prince Bertie.

"Look who I ran into on my way back!"

Rex bowed his head while Dora rose from her chair. She made to curtsy, but Prince Bertie stopped her before she could.

"None of that, please. I insist. I don't want to interrupt your evening, but when Clark mentioned you were here, I thought it was a sign of good fortune."

Dora and Rex exchanged glances. "How is that?" Rex asked. "Do you need something from us?"

"It's the opposite, but now isn't the appropriate time for such a discussion. Might you be free to visit me tomorrow? Say two in the afternoon?"

"Of course, your highness," Dora replied. They finished by sending their regards to Lady Elizabeth. All the while, Dora's mind was spinning.

The question of what Bertie meant with his remark kept her occupied for the rest of the night. She kept a bright smile plastered to her face and squealed with delight when Clark accepted their invitation, but underneath, she did nothing but fret.

What kind of gift did Bertie think to bestow? Honours and attention of that sort were the last things Dora needed. It was imperative that she and Rex be able to depart for their next adventure without the world thinking they were bosom buddies with the crown.

She broached the topic with Rex when they turned in. He was much less concerned.

"Whatever it is, we'll deal with it, Dora," he said before kissing her goodnight.

That night, it was her time to toss and turn.

She didn't begrudge Rex his peaceful slumber. He had yet to experience the darker side of being a spy. When they arrived in Rome, he'd soon see how hard it was to disguise one's loyalty. Oddly enough, the world would be happier imagining Prince Edward or Prince Bertie as another one of Theodora's conquests.

But conquests didn't get rewarded or invited to state events.

As awkward as it might be, Dora decided she'd decline such an honour, should it be offered. She'd play dumb, or employ some other technique to cover the faux pas of offending a royal. Better that than the alternative.

At two PM, Dora laced her fingers through Rex's and walked beside him into the side entrance of Buckingham Palace. The prince's private secretary led them along hushed corridors. The nameplates on the closed doors identified the rooms as private offices for the staff. It was an unusual place for a prince to entertain guests.

Dora had no idea what to make of that.

The secretary, a discreet chap of a similar age to the prince, opened the door marked with his name and bid them to go in. "If you wouldn't mind waiting here, his highness will be right with you."

He closed the door behind himself, remaining outside.

The room was simply furnished with a wooden desk, matching chair, and two seats for visitors. Dora chose one while Rex sat in the other. The room didn't even have a window.

There was nothing to see, but a few framed certificates hung on the wall, noting the secretary's achievements.

Dora tamped the temptation to rifle through the desk drawers, but it was a near thing. If they'd been anywhere else in the world, she'd have told Rex to guard the door while she had a peek.

Prince Bertie arrived before her resolve failed. Again, he motioned for them to keep their seats. He circled around the desk and settled into his secretary's chair.

Dora kept perfectly still as he crossed his hands and rested them on the desk. The scene had shades of being called into the headteacher's office. She was no longer sure why they were there. Had she misinterpreted his words?

He did not leave her to wait overlong.

Prince Bertie spoke carefully, taking time to say each word. "There is one distinct advantage to being the son of the king. As a royal highness, I have the right to make demands of those below me in rank. It is not a right I use often, but this time, I made an exception."

Made? Of whom?

"Following the events of the previous month, I indicated my intention to reward your valour to Lord Audley. I presumed he'd suggest something appropriate. Instead, he insisted I do no such thing."

Dora caught her breath. What had Audley done? Why hadn't he warned her? Was this repayment for her trick of asking forgiveness instead of permission?

"He made every attempt to fob off my queries. I had no choice but to threaten him in turn. If there was something amiss with your actions, he had no right to keep me from the truth."

Dora's veins turned to ice. Surely Audley wouldn't reveal her secret.

"Miss Laurent, I do not know your name. At that, Lord

Audley drew a line. He professed his willingness to hang rather than reveal your secrets. But he left me with no question as to your allegiance to this country and the throne. Your reasons for doing his bidding remain your own."

Dora inclined her head in thanks.

"Lord Rex, you are well known and well respected by all. Still, Lord Audley insisted you'd shy away from a reward for solving Hugh's murder. Is this true?"

Rex didn't hesitate. "It is, your highness. I acted out of duty to my friend as much as to help you."

Prince Bertie narrowed his gaze, studying Rex's face. "True, and yet I have the sense you've left something out. So be it. I am aware you are due to leave our shores in the near future. Before you go, I'd like to extend an offer. If there is anything I can do, anything within my power, or that of my father, please ask. I insist. My debt to you for saving Elizabeth's life weighs upon my shoulders. It would be my genuine pleasure to repay it."

Rex answered with the appropriate remarks, thanking Bertie for his gesture, but insisting again it wasn't necessary.

Dora should have been doing the same.

But, in the back of her mind, an idea blossomed.

She had everything she could ever want — freedom, love, adventure — but there was someone else in her life who yearned for more.

For that person, that dear, most special companion, she would throw aside her tendency to abstain from reward.

Without consulting any of the parties involved, she steadied her nerves and made her request.

Dora dropped her French facade. In a crisp British accent, she said, "There is one thing you could do for me, your highness. It is highly irregular, perhaps even illegal, but it isn't immoral. That much I can promise. There is one impossible thing I want, and your father is the only person in the world capable of making it happen."

Dora ignored Rex's gaping mouth as he stared at the side of her face. She didn't move her gaze from Prince Bertie.

He cocked his head to the side, this time studying her. Whatever he saw, it must have mollified his concerns.

"Tell me, Miss Laurent. What is it you desire?"

"A wedding."

Epilogue

I nga stepped back from the mirror and smoothed her hands over her hips. She turned one way, and then the other, examining how the silk dress fell over her curves.

It was hardly the first time she'd donned a posh frock. In Dora's early days, Inga had often accompanied her to balls and galas. It was only after Harris came into their lives that she chose to remain more often at home.

On the rare occasions she ventured out, she was happy enough to wear an old dress. It wasn't due to any lack of funds. She simply had minimal interest in fashion, and even less so in keeping up with the trends.

She'd always been this way. Her father would undoubtedly blame it on Inga's lack of a proper mother-figure in her life. She'd had nannies and her dear, sweet Oma to shower her with affection. But no one could ever take the place of a mother in a girl's heart.

Instead of spending her pennies on hair ribbons or stealing glances at her mother's magazines, Inga had studied the man's world. She'd noted how people stepped aside for her father.

She'd seen the scores of men working in his office. She didn't miss the lack of female figures there, either.

That was okay, she'd assured herself. When she grew up, she'd take her place at her father's side. She'd hire more women to sit beside her.

As far as dreams went, it was well and good. That is, until her father caught wind of her future plans.

"Absolutely not!" he'd cried. "Don't you see, child! I built all of this so that you'd never have to lift a hand. So that you can marry and bless me with grandchildren in return."

He'd meant well, but knowing that didn't soften the blow. Most young women would have abandoned their childish thoughts and fallen into line. Inga, however, was not one of them.

She funnelled her pocket money into feminist causes until the war broke out. Then she'd lobbied her father until he agreed to fund her place as a nurse. Likely, he'd thought that the realities of war would send her scurrying back to his side.

Instead, in the former seaside village of Le Touquet, Miss Inga Kay found herself sharing a room with Lady Dorothy Cavendish. The rest, as they say, was history.

They abandoned the idea of a normal life and pursued the thrill of being undercover spies. Even in the darkest hours of the night, the women had never dreamed of someday marrying. Of settling down. Of spending the rest of their days with the same man.

Yet, here Inga stood, studying her wedding dress in her bedroom mirror. Every decision that had led to this moment had been her own.

It should be the happiest day of her life. And it was... even so, something was off.

Inga pressed her hands to her waist and took a deep breath. The v-shaped crease between her eyebrows didn't move.

The bedroom door opened, and Dora stepped inside. She caught sight of Inga's expression in the mirror. "You don't like the dress?"

"No. The dress is fine," Inga answered.

"The shoes? Your hair?" Dora walked around Inga, studying her with a critical eye. "Is it the earrings? I know you prefer studs, but this dress requires something bolder."

"There isn't anything wrong with any of it, Dora," Inga assured her. She wasn't lying. The issue wasn't with the choice of clothing or any of the accessories. What weighed upon her was guilt.

Quite simply, Inga and Harris were getting married. Dora and Rex were not.

Inga didn't know how to square that fact in her mind. Dora and Rex were no less committed to one another. Yet, without even a moment of hesitation, Dora had thrown away her one chance to wed in order to make marriage possible for Inga.

It was an enormous gift, with no strings attached, paid in full by Dora's unwavering and deep, abiding friendship with Inga.

How did one go about saying thank you for a sacrifice of that magnitude?

Inga didn't need to pose the question. She and Dora had been friends for so long that the other woman was practically capable of reading her mind.

Dora threw her arm around Inga's waist and hugged her tight. "Don't you dare be sad today, do you hear me? No what ifs or might have beens. I have everything I ever wanted, and a million times more. This was one small thing I could do for you. Accept it."

Inga laid her hand over Dora's. She looked into the mirror, meeting Dora's emerald eyes in the reflection. The two women looked nothing alike — one blonde and the other brunette, their shapes as different as their personalities. And yet, they were closer than most sisters.

Dora scrunched her nose and then stuck out her tongue, ruining her glamorous facade. Inga was helpless against the ridiculous scene. Her desperate attempts to keep a serious expression ended with her snorting in laughter.

"There now, that's better. If you walk down the aisle with that dour expression on your face, Harris is going to think you're having second thoughts."

"If he's wearing one of his more colourful vests under his new suit, it would serve him right if I left him there all alone."

Dora wagged a finger at Inga. "Please! You know you love his quirks as much as his handsome face. Enough of the shenanigans. We have more important things to discuss."

Inga raised an eyebrow. "Such as?"

Dora wiped all amusement from her face until she was the very picture of innocence. "We should discuss what happens on the wedding night. I wouldn't want you to be unprepared." She fluttered her lashes.

Inga swatted her on the arm. "You're dreadful. Do you know that?"

"I do try..." Dora confessed. "I received a call from Tabitha while you were bathing. As we guessed, she's expecting. Her little bundle will arrive this summer. If you and Harris get a move on, your children can be playmates."

Inga blanched. "There are so many things wrong with that statement that I don't know where to begin. Wait, yes I do. There will be no wedding night babies. And even if there were — which there will not be — he or she would hardly be an appropriate playmate for the child of Lady Tabitha FitzClarence."

"The world is changing, Inga," Dora countered. "Little by little, every single day. You and I are partially responsible. Who knows what society will deem acceptable in five, ten, or twenty years' time."

Inga's mind wandered into the future. She had seen so much progress in her lifetime. Yet, there was always room for more. Maybe society would change enough to allow Reginald Bankes-Fernsby and Theodora Laurent to wed, as well.

Or maybe it wouldn't.

That was the worry that lingered in the back of Inga's mind. She did her best to quash that voice as she finished her toilette and let Dora smooth her hair. But that flicker of hope, that someday might become one day, refused to let go.

"Come along, Inga. If we don't leave now, we'll be late getting to the Archbishop's office. You know just how many strings I had to pull to arrange for a private ceremony with him. If we don't show up on time, we may never get a second chance."

Dora walked ahead of Inga as they descended the stairs. Archie was waiting out back with the car motor running. Cynthia helped both women into their coats and passed them their handbags. Basel held the door open.

Inga made it three steps outside before her feet refused to go another.

"What's wrong now?" Dora asked.

"I forgot something upstairs. I'll only be a moment. Wait here."

Inga rushed back into the house. She bypassed the stairs and went straight for the telephone in the study.

There were rules for how and when they were allowed to contact Lord Audley.

Inga ignored all of them. She gave his number to the operator and begged the woman to hurry. She issued the same command again when his lordship's butler answered the line.

Audley's voice was laced with worry when he picked up the phone. "What's happened?"

Inga wasted no time. Any moment now, Dora could walk through the back door and demand to know what she was doing. She didn't bother framing her request as anything other than a command. She ended it with a question.

"Will you do this for me?"

"Of course," he answered, just as forthright in his reply.

Inga replaced the earpiece and leaned against the wall, allowing herself a single moment to catch her breath.

From outside, the horn of Dora's Mercedes-Benz blared three times in fast repetition.

Inga took her sweet time going outside. She demanded Archie adopt a sedate pace in the car, stating she didn't want to muss her hair with any of his hairpin turns.

Dora rolled her eyes, not bothering to cover her annoyance. But this was Inga's big day. She wouldn't deny the woman any request, no matter how outlandish it might be.

That was what Inga was counting on.

And so they were late. Five full minutes, as Dora was quick to point out.

Inga didn't care. "It's my wedding day. I've waited long enough for it to arrive. Now that it's here, a few minutes more or less won't make any difference."

She kept a serene smile on her face despite the boldfaced lies slipping from her lips. Inga needed every spare minute she could get if her plan was going to have a chance at success.

"Let's go through the church," she suggested. Dressed as they were in their finery, Inga and Dora joined the line of people waiting to enter Westminster Abbey. Their winter coats covered most of their dresses. No one was looking at them, anyway. There was far too much richness for the eyes to feast on inside the building.

Inga followed the signs to the front of the church. She took a moment to take in the final resting place of Elizabeth I. Even Dora grew quiet, out of respect for the extraordinary woman. Next, Inga ventured past the Cosmati pavement upon which so many of England's rulers had received their crowns.

It was that relationship between monarch and church that made Inga's wedding possible. As head of the Church of England, King George had the ability to sign off on a secret wedding between spies, where one was living under an assumed name. With his blessing, they'd skipped past the obligatory posting of the banns. The Archbishop of Canterbury himself would conduct the ceremony far from the gaze of prying eyes. The marriage license would remain a secret.

Inga gave silent thanks to everyone on earth and above who had made this day possible.

Dora coughed politely and pointed at her wrist. They needed to move.

Inga joined her friend's stride without complaining as they hurried to the private office where the Archbishop, Harris, and Rex awaited.

They found the door easily enough. Inga grabbed Dora's arm and spun her around before she could go in. She scanned Dora from head to toe. "You'll do."

"I'll do for what?" Dora asked, completely thrown by the unexpected comment.

Inga stepped around her and opened the door. The first person she saw was Harris.

His bald head gleamed under the electric lights. His wide smile shone even brighter.

Inga didn't even care about the rose-coloured vest peeking out from his coat.

Next, she saw Rex. He, too, grinned from ear-to-ear. Like

Dora, he was thrilled to share in the celebration of their matrimony.

"Where's the Archbishop? Did we miss him?" Dora asked, leaning around Inga to search the small office.

"He's running behind," Harris assured her. "Some last-minute visitor, or so his secretary explained."

Inga crossed the room and held out a hand. Harris grasped it and squeezed tight. If he was nervous, he showed no sign of it. Neither did she.

Inga Kay had never felt more at peace in her life.

Dora sidled up to Rex and slipped her arm through his. Together, they all turned around at the sound of the doorknob.

The first man to enter was the Archbishop. Inga had never met the man in person, but she recognised his face from photos in the paper.

She heard Dora gasp when someone followed him through the door.

"Lord Audley?" Dora blurted, forgetting to use her fake French accent.

"I'm not here to intrude," he assured her. "I'm here to act as the witness."

Dora's brows slanted in confusion. "Rex and I are the witnesses."

"I'm aware that was the plan, but things have changed," he said, as though his words offered some kind of illumination.

They didn't. Not to Dora, anyway. But Inga understood.

The Archbishop smiled benevolently at Inga and Harris. "With the blessing of his royal highness, King George V, I am here to offer the sacrament of holy matrimony. I understand you wish to undertake this sacrament, and to join your lives together from now into eternity. Is that correct?"

"It is," they replied in unison.

"Excellent. Lord Audley, my friend of many years, came to

me with a question. In light of the unusual circumstances, and in recognition of sacrifices made for the sake of the realm, might I be willing to make a small change to the plan?" The Archbishop looked first at Inga and then back to Lord Audley. "To his request, I could only agree. If they are ready and willing, I will do so."

"Do what?" Dora asked, her voice laced with worry. The poor dear was so rarely thrown for a loop that she had no idea how to act. Patience, it seemed, eluded her.

With great satisfaction, and no small amount of pride, Lord Audley answered her question.

"Dora and Rex, my request was this. If the Archbishop can conduct one secret wedding today, is there any reason he can't conduct two? In anticipation of your response, I present myself here to act as your witness."

Rex froze in place. Not out of fear so much as disbelief. He had the look of a child at Christmas, discovering every outlandish gift request had been fulfilled.

Dora's wide-eyed gaze shifted right to Inga's face. Her mouth half-open. Her body completely still.

Inga tossed her a cheeky smile. "As I said, Dora. You'll do. You'll both do just fine. All you have to say is yes."

* * *

Want more Dora and Rex? They will be back in **The Roman Riddle**.

A race against time to uncover the truth, with the future of an old friend at stake.

Rome, 1923. Rex and Dora's holiday comes to an abrupt end

when they receive an urgent message from Rome. The Carabinieri have arrested the British ambassador.

The charge is murder. The ambassador is Dora's old friend.

The victim — a young woman — is unidentified.

An eyewitness puts the ambassador at the scene and the evidence points to his guilt. But if the Carabinieri are wrong, this simple case will become an international incident.

Rex and Dora face their most difficult puzzle yet. First, they have to identify the victim. Only then can they determine who had the motive to kill.

But in the Eternal City, the past and present are intertwined. Old flames return, past grudges reemerge, and regrets bring consequences. Before the case ends, they'll have to answer a riddle. What is more important — solving the case or saving the life of a friend?

Find out in **The Roman Riddle**. Order your copy now on Amazon.

* * *

Want to keep updated on my newest books? Subscribe to my newsletter for book news, sales, special offers, and great reading recommendations. You can sign up here: lynnmorrison. myflodesk.com/dcd-newsletter

Historical Notes

My planning process for each Dora and Rex book begins the same way — with me searching through the timeline for an interesting historical event. When my eyes landed on a royal engagement and wedding in early 1923, I knew I'd found my place to start.

There was plenty of fuel for inspiration in the historical record. By now, we all know what a seminal event it was when Prince Albert married Lady Elizabeth Bowes-Lyon. They'd go on to become King George VI and Queen Elizabeth, later the Queen Mother. We've read stories and seen portrayals of the king's work to overcome his stutter so he could later lead a nation at war. Certainly, Queen Elizabeth II's dedication to crown and country came in large part through the teachings of her parents.

But in 1923, Prince Albert, known to friends as Bertie, was the reticent younger brother. Prince Edward, playboy and society darling, was expected to inherit the throne from his father. He did... albeit for a short time, before abdicating to wed American divorcée Wallis Simpson.

Looking back, it is ironic that it was Prince Albert's choice of bride that originally raised eyebrows. As told in my story, Prince Albert proposed to Lady Elizabeth no less than three times before she agreed to become his wife. She had an incredible fear of losing herself and her voice entirely if she became part of the royal clan. It took a visit from Queen Mary to convince the young woman to change her mind.

Although Queen Mary was sure Elizabeth was the right woman for her Bertie, society was less confident in the choice. Lady Elizabeth's bloodlines were a paler shade of blue. Her father was a lowly Earl and with a Scottish title to boot. Princes were expected to marry princesses.

While some viewed Albert's choice to marry 'below him' as a welcome modernisation for the stuffy crown, others were less convinced. It was this tidbit that I used as the foundation for my mystery. While I'd like to say for certain that the closest friends of the real Prince Albert supported his decision, having them do otherwise made for a more interesting story.

I hope you will forgive me for taking such liberties!

This is the first book where I allowed some of the actual Bright Young People to make a cameo. I underestimated the challenge of writing their style of parties into a cozy read. The Strachey brothers and their friends like Cecil Beaton and Nancy Mitford didn't walk on the wild side. They ran all over it. The only taboo was acting conservatively. I have full faith in Rex's and Dora's abilities to keep up with the crowd, but poor Benedict! He'd have absolutely been over his head. That's why I decided to move their interview with Rupert over to a more sedate scene.

Rupert's tale of an Australian dalliance also took inspiration from another real event. Prior to proposing to Lady Elizabeth, Prince Albert had his sights on a married Australian socialite named Lady Longborough. Christened as Sheila Chisholm, she is widely viewed as the reason why the phrase 'A good-looking Sheila' came to be adopted as Australian slang.

With Prince Edward courting her best friend, Sheila found herself in close quarters with Prince Albert. Prince Edward observed the clear chemistry between them and orchestrated a way for Sheila's husband to leave the house, allowing Bertie to succumb to his desires. After Bertie and Sheila became a couple, the foursome spent so much time together that they called themselves 'The Four Do's' as in the Derring Do's.

You can imagine King George V's reaction when he discovered both his heir-apparent and the spare were courting unhappily married women. Prince Albert buckled under his father's threats and abandoned any plans he had to settle down with Sheila in the longer term. Not long after, he met Lady Elizabeth for the first time.

Although a century has passed since the Bright Young Things raced their cars around London, causing havoc wherever they went, society hasn't really moved that far. The current heir married a commoner, of all things, raising many eyebrows. And the spare is living in California after marrying a divorcée. In 1922, Lady Elizabeth feared she'd lose her freedom to speak and act under the restrictions of the royal family. In 2023, the girlfriends and later wives of the current princes expressed similar sentiments.

Despite the flow of time, the press is still quick to issue pronouncements about who is and is not acceptable as a royal bride. Society still argues over the right and wrongness of the private choices of these men. Plots abound, secrets get leaked, friendships ebb and flow.

As the French say: *Plus ça change, plus c'est la même chose.* Life goes on, but somehow is ever more of the same.

Acknowledgments

While writing this book, circumstances demanded I do so without ready access to my laptop. I dictated what I could, and hand-wrote much of the rest. By the time I reached The End, I had three notebooks filled with my scribbles... and no idea how I was going to get them typed, edited, and ready to publish.

That's when my parents stepped in. A humongous thank you goes to my father and mother, Ken and Joyce Morrison, for offering a hand when I needed one most. Even though they say a parent's work is never done, I'm sure they thought that by the time I hit my 40s, they'd get a break. Sorry for that!

Thank you to Anne Radcliffe for providing expert support while I was plotting. I very much appreciate Brenda Chapman, Fiona Birchall, and Ewa Bartnik for beta reading. They provided great feedback, despite the horrors of typos and grammatical errors still dotting the pages.

I must give a shout-out to the amazing authors who cheered me on this year. From my cool cozy gang to the FAKAs to the old and new friends I saw at conferences - THANK YOU! Between our ongoing chats and daily writing sprints, I never feel like writing is a solitary enterprise.

To all my readers who get in touch, either in my Facebook reader group or via email, your support means the world to me. It never fails that on the days that are the hardest, an expected message arrives to brighten my outlook.

The Roman Riddle
A Dora and Rex 1920s Mystery

A race against time to uncover the truth, with the future of an old friend at stake.

Rome, 1923. Rex and Dora's holiday comes to an abrupt end when they receive an urgent message from Rome. The Carabinieri have arrested the British ambassador.

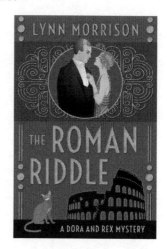

The charge is murder. The ambassador is Dora's old friend.

The victim -- a young woman -- is unidentified.

An eyewitness puts the ambassador at the scene and the evidence points to his guilt. But if the Carabinieri are wrong, this simple case will become an international incident.

Rex and Dora face their most difficult puzzle yet. First, they have to identify the victim. Only then can they determine who had the motive to kill.

But in the Eternal City, the past and present are intertwined. Old flames return, past grudges reemerge, and regrets bring consequences. Before the case ends, they'll have to answer a riddle. What is more important -- solving the case or saving the life of a friend?

Find out in **The Roman Riddle**. Order your copy now on Amazon.

About the Author

Lynn Morrison lives in Oxford, England along with her husband, two daughters and two cats. Born and raised in Mississippi, her wanderlust attitude has led her to live in California, Italy, France, the UK, and the Netherlands. Despite having rubbed shoulders with presidential candidates and members of parliament, night-clubbed in Geneva and Prague, explored Japanese temples and scrambled through Roman ruins, Lynn's real life adventures can't compete with the stories in her mind.

She is as passionate about reading as she is writing, and can almost always be found with a book in hand. You can find out more about her on her website LynnMorrisonWriter.com.

You can chat with her directly in her Facebook group - Lynn Morrison's Not a Book Club - where she talks about books, life and anything else that crosses her mind.

facebook.com/nomadmomdiary

instagram.com/nomadmomdiary

bookbub.com/authors/lynn-morrison

goodreads.com/nomadmomdiary

amazon.com/Lynn-Morrison/e/B00IKC1LVW

Also by Lynn Morrison

Raven's Matriarch

Raven's Storm

Wandering Witch Urban Fantasy

A Queen Only Lives Twice

Made in the USA
Middletown, DE
07 November 2023

42132020R00139